Praise for *A Free State*

"Astonishing. . . . This beautiful writing finds echoes in conflicts that persist—envy, imitation, injustice, brutality, inequality—and ultimately offers hope. I urge you to read it for yourself."
—Elvis Costello

"Both a literary thriller and a meditation on the complexities and contradictions of America's cultural heritage . . . includes fascinating nuggets of musical history and period detail."
—*The New Yorker*

"The story of an escaped slave banjo genius who gets a brief gig in a blackface minstrel show in Philadelphia while pursued by a vicious bounty hunter. Nothing rolls out just as you'd expect. . . . It reads like magic. Just riveting."
—Barry Mazor

"A fascinating study on the nature of freedom in the guise of a thought-provoking novel."
—*Clarion-Ledger* (Jackson, Miss.)

"Like a Delta bluesman, Tom Piazza sings about the United States in terms of love and loss and heartbreak. . . . The America of *A Free State* remains sadly recognizable, a place of reckless beauty too often overshadowed by ideological duplicity and internecine violence."
—Sean Kinch, *Chapter 16*

"A passionate and timely novel . . . orchestrates themes of violence, entrapment, and loyalty to draw the twenty-first-century reader into pre–Civil War struggles of life and death—conflicts which resonate still in today's world of racial profiling and invisible white privilege. The novel interlaces literary artistry with a heart-pumping narrative pace." —*Chattanooga Pulse*

"A thrilling pursuit adventure. But the action of *A Free State* conceals a deeper purpose, which is to probe, through the medium of nineteenth-century minstrelsy, elaborate contradictions in the antebellum psyche."
—*Atlanta Journal-Constitution*

"Brilliant. . . . *A Free State* is the taut yet expansive complement to *Huckleberry Finn* that we have long been in need of. But the resolution of Twain's masterpiece is a drag. The last leap of *A Free State* . . . I won't spoil it." —Roy Blount, Jr.

"Tom Piazza's new novel is a crisply told tale of race relations in Philadelphia a few years before the Civil War, one that brings into sharp relief the tensions that beset Northern society even as it was about to go to war to rid the nation of slavery." —*BookPage*

"A page-turning novel about real times that are stranger than fiction." —*New York Post*

A FREE
STATE

ALSO BY TOM PIAZZA

The Southern Journey of Alan Lomax

Devil Sent the Rain

City of Refuge

Why New Orleans Matters

Understanding Jazz

My Cold War

True Adventures with the King of Bluegrass

Blues Up and Down

Setting the Tempo (editor)

Blues and Trouble

The Guide to Classic Recorded Jazz

HARPER ● PERENNIAL

NEW YORK ● LONDON ● TORONTO ● SYDNEY ● NEW DELHI ● AUCKLAND

A FREE STATE

A NOVEL

TOM PIAZZA

HARPER PERENNIAL

A hardcover edition of this book was published in 2015 by HarperCollins Publishers.

HarperCollins books may be purchased for educational, business, or sales promotional use. For information, please e-mail the Special Markets Department at SPsales@harpercollins.com.

FIRST HARPER PERENNIAL EDITION PUBLISHED 2016.

Designed by Michael Correy

Library of Congress Cataloging-in-Publication Data has been applied for.

ISBN 978-0-06-228413-6 (pbk.)

16 17 18 19 20   OV/RRD   10 9 8 7 6 5 4 3 2 1

FOR MARY

I was a derision to all my people; and *their song all the day.*

—LAMENTATIONS 3:14

PART
I

1

City haze shot through with morning sun. Buildings razed, buildings rising, dust drifting off the dirt streets drying in the morning air. Clank of carts on cobblestones, barrels unloaded, the men shouting, the mist burning off the river. Along Chestnut, along Walnut, along Market, they make their way, amid hollering and hammering and the smell of horse and mule shit. Open doors to taverns, men in bowler hats, bricks and shingles and the cart at the curb. The street sloping down toward the river and the docks.

Henry Sims regarded the poster as people jostled past on the sidewalk:

$200 REWARD!
RANAWAY FROM THE SUBSCRIBER, AT THE TIDES, FAIRHOPE, VIRGINIA, ONE NEGRO, JOSEPH, AGED 19, 5 FEET AND 7 INCHES IN HEIGHT; IS OF A LIGHT COPPER COLOR WITH GREEN EYES, CLEVER AND PERSONABLE, AN EXCELLENT MIMIC; MAY WELL BE

TRYING TO PASS AS SPANISH OR AS FREEMAN. VERY PROFICIENT
PERFORMER ON THE BANJAR. HAD ON WHEN LAST SEEN, ROUGH
BROWN TROUSERS, WHITE DRESS SHIRT, A BLUE JACKET AND
PAIR OF NEW HUNTING BOOTS BELONGING TO THE UNDERSIGNED.
LIKELY HEADED FOR CINCINNATI, BOSTON, PHILADELPHIA, OR
NEW YORK. A REWARD OF $200 WILL BE GIVEN UPON HIS
DELIVERY TO HIS RIGHTFUL OWNER. JAMES STEPHENS, THE TIDES,
FAIRHOPE, VIRGINIA.

In the upper-right-hand corner, the silhouetted runaway, the shouldered stick with the bundle on the end, the frightened, caricatured black face. Not much of a likeness, he thought. In the distance, the river, steaming and shivering in the light morning breeze.

Three months earlier, Henry, born Joseph, had noticed a version of the same poster, offering $150. He was, apparently, rising in his former master's esteem. Over the weeks, that poster faded and tore and was covered by others. Every vertical surface in Philadelphia was a riot of posters and handbills crowing and cajoling, some fresh and sharp, some buckling and peeling like birch bark, announcing performances by operatic artists, contortionists, orators, Shakespearean companies, comedic sketches, dramas at the Chestnut Street Theater, all competing for space and attention with the reward posters for those who, like himself, had made their way out of what the solemn members of the Vigilance Committee liked to call the House of Bondage.

He turned his attention to a larger poster, adjacent.

HELD OVER!!

AT

BARTON'S MINSTREL THEATER

THE ORIGINAL

VIRGINIA HARMONISTS

PURVEYORS OF ETHIOPIAN AIRS

PLANTATION JIGS

AND EVERY VARIETY OF

NEGRO JOLLITY

MESSRS. POWELL AND

DOUGLASS ON THE ENDS

UNRIVALLED HILARITY

MR. MULLIGAN WILL PERFORM HIS

SPECIALTY

"FIRE DOWN BELOW"

NIGHTLY

PERFORMANCES COMMENCE

AT 7 O'CLOCK

PUNCTUALLY

Above the text, an engraved depiction of five figures with black faces, seated in a semicircle, limbs jutting and jabbing, playing banjo, fiddle, tambourine, a set of bones. The troupes, in which white men blackened their faces with burnt cork and sang and played like Negroes, were beyond number, and popular beyond measure. The Virginia Minstrels, the Sable Harmonists, the Christy Minstrels, Sanford's Minstrels, the Ethiopian Serenaders. Plantation Melodies, African Extempore, Essence of Old Virginny, Zip Coon, Jim Crow, Take Me Back to Dixie's Land . . .

No, Henry thought—take me not back to Dixie's Land. You can have Dixie's Land.

He hefted the sack in his hand, felt the light weight of the banjo with pleasure. Time, he thought, to purvey some Ethiopian airs. On a bright morning such as this he was still astonished at the feeling. To walk where you want to walk, as a free man. To look at the sunlight on the side of a brick building as a free man, to smell bread baking as a free man. To touch a tree, to tie your boot on the sidewalk, to enter a tavern, free. To know yourself to be more capable than most of the white men who, even here, condescend to you, and to be able to show it without fear of a whipping. To climb the stairs, to feel money in your pocket, as a free man. That was worth everything.

He turned and started down Walnut Street, toward the river. Like all musicians, he loved a river.

2

first saw Henry Sims on the corner of Chestnut and Front Streets, performing for the lunchtime idlers. He wore a bright-red flannel shirt buttoned at the neck despite the warm spring day, black suspenders, and a dark-gold, shallow-crowned straw hat which sat well back on his head, giving the impression of a halo.

That afternoon I was on my way to a dry goods shop where the troupe got fabrics at a discount. Powell had worked up a fem routine that we were planning to insert at the beginning of the evening's second half, and I was going to purchase some crinolines that Rose had requested. In addition to my role as Brother Neckbones, I had installed myself as our manager, accountant, property master, and, importantly, costume consultant, in no small part because it gave me ongoing reason to have business with Rose.

I heard the sound of the banjo before I saw its source. The song was recognizable as "Old Dan Tucker," but the tune was surrounded by a rowdy chorus of other tunes and half-tunes, banjo voices and lines of notes, all of which seemed to comment upon the main melody in tones of mockery, qualification, and encouragement.

I assumed there were at least two men playing, but as I approached the edge of the small crowd I saw a solitary, light-skinned Negro who was not only playing the banjo but dancing as well. The upper part of his body remained still except for his hands, but from hips to ground his legs had an independent life, shuttling from one position to another, in constant motion except for brief moments when he would hold still, as if daring you to fix his image in your mind. All the while he maintained a calm, enigmatic smile, as if he were merely sitting on a riverbank, watching the boats pass by.

Every one of us in the Virginia Harmonists had made it a point to study as many Colored musicians as we could track down. We were scholars of a sort: we conducted our studies in fields, in barns, on cabin porches, and on the docks. Yet I had never seen anything like what I was witnessing. Others played their instruments, with large or modest skill; perhaps they danced or sang or delivered a fragmentary monologue. But here was a true performer, in absolute command of his audience's attention. His little dance figures mimicked the turns of the melody and rhythm, as well as the substance of the lyrics. When he sang

> *Combed his hair with a wagon wheel*
> *And died with a toothache in his heel . . .*

he executed a maneuver with his ankles that made it appear as if the ground were sliding away under his feet. Arriving at the song's refrain,

Get out the way, Old Dan Tucker . . .

he would spring abruptly to one side with no apparent exertion, to the crowd's audible delight.

It was impossible to turn away. This, I realized immediately, was what we needed. I listened to him sing and play three songs, until he removed the straw hat from his head with a flourish, made a bow, and solicited contributions.

"I'm not the preacher," he announced, setting his hat down on the cobblestones, "and I'm not the preacher's son—but I'll take up collection 'til the preacher comes . . ." Five or six coins fell under his glance as he twisted a tuning peg, thumbing a string, repeatedly, as its pitch rose and took its proper place in the choir. I remember the sharp sunlight and the rushing clouds on that brilliant, blustery afternoon.

I hung back to let the crowd disperse, meaning to talk to him in private. As I waited, my attention was distracted for a moment by some barrels falling off the back of a cart and making an ungodly racket, which startled everyone. When I turned my attention back to the group, the wizard had disappeared. Not a sign of him, as if he were a djinn returned to a bottle and spirited away. It was the first evidence I had of his genius for escape. I swore that I would return and find out who he was. And that is what changed everything for me.

* * *

I had been in Philadelphia for three years.

I had made a place, and a name, for myself in that sprawling city, with its alleys and avenues, its great stone churches and its mean dockside hotels, its Southwark and its Callowhill and its broad public squares. At that time it was hard to know whether the city was under construction or demolition. It was, in fact, both, and at a feverish pace. The same might have been said for the entire nation. Buildings, businesses, whole communities sprang up seemingly overnight, then were torn down to make way for their successors, as if living out some myth of endless progress, of clear title to reshape the world day to day.

At least this was the case in the Northern states. In the South, a different myth was under construction—of some fancied Golden Age, a glorious past built on the bones of the present, some vision of columned buildings and millennial stasis. A stage setting, behind which you could hear the groans of the dark-skinned men and women who labored without pay to keep the illusion inflated. It was an odd spectacle to witness at a distance, especially for those who were raised in the illusion-free setting of a small working farm holding, as I had been, and who supplied the necessary labor themselves.

My grandparents on either side had arrived in America during the first great wave of Irish immigration, sometime soon after the nation had become a nation, and they settled near the Pennsylvania borderlands, not far from what became Gettysburg. My father's line of Scotch-Irish mistrusted the cities, mistrusted in fact any form of imagination beyond what was necessary to establish one's own holding and be left alone. My mother was Catholic Irish, and so nothing if not imaginative, and life in my father's literal and figurative Presbyterian gristmill must have been a kind of slow extinction. I saw this, although none of my ten siblings—all of whom were older than myself—seemed to, and I was always trying to raise a smile on her face with some little song or saying.

I was beaten regularly. All my brothers were beaten, although my eldest brothers seemed to take it as a badge of pride and a token of affection. I did not. If ever my father saw me idle, or enjoying a joke or a game of my own devising, this was cause for correction. A smell of stale urine and perspiration came off him as he whipped me with a doubled length of rope and an expressionless face. It was the closest physical contact I had with him. I did not wish for more.

Oddly enough, my father did not mind music. He played the fiddle in a flatfooted, unadorned manner, and he had a number of the old ballads by heart, things such as "The Unquiet Grave" and "The Twa' Corbies." His ordinarily watchful, squinting eyes would close and his brows arch slightly when he would approach one of the higher melody notes. I found these songs rather somber, but I was fascinated by the very fact that they existed—that a person, even one as stolid as my father, could all but change shape by shifting from the spoken language of workaday concern into song, as if stepping through a window onto the moon.

As soon as I was deemed old enough—five years old—I was delegated to drag sacks of this or that over here or there, under the low wood rafters, and to stand by a cart until brother Mac returned, and to milk our cows when sister Margaret had other responsibilities. My father grudgingly allowed me to attend school—at my mother's insistence—

and I had instruction until the age of eleven, at which time I was officially herded toward the waiting yoke. Not even the mill, but rather some dismal farmland he had acquired, half a day's ride away, near Carlisle.

It broke my heart to leave my mother. She was my refuge from an oppressive tedium—the dispenser of consoling words, little rhymes, small tokens always hidden from my father and brothers, such as a piece of pie or candy that she had acquired somehow. I suppose I was her refuge as well. She wept when I left. I did as well, but I did it out of sight.

At the farm, I worked under the supervision of my brothers Duncan and Robert. They took after our father in their habits. The days were intolerably long, and filled with pointless repetitive labor. Work this pump until your right arm drops off. Repeat, with your left, until you are armless. Sleep upon a horsehair pallet half an inch thick, grow two arms back, repeat the next day. Grind this, lift this, carry this, pull this. My brothers, never warm to begin with, were strangers to me now, whose only means of social intercourse seemed to be the shouting of orders, the emission of rude jokes, and the administration of physical punishment, with and without cause. I had no privacy whatsoever, except for Sundays after church, when I would steal a precious hour or two and escape into the one book I had managed to export from home— *Robinson Crusoe*.

I hated the farm, and I thought my life had ended prematurely, but it was there that I first saw the Negro minstrels.

My brothers had met two sisters in the town, a brewer's daughters as I remember, and invited them to a show which was to be held in a tent on a neighboring farm. At that time, and in that place, entertainment was not easily available, and when some itinerant offering came through, whether it was a lantern show or a lecture or a circus, everyone attended.

Of course my brothers had no inclination to bring me along on their evening of courtship, but I put up a racket, threatening every type of insurrection—I was twelve years old, and I could have brought the farm's gears to a halt in half a dozen ways—and they gave in, installing me in the rear of a cart, amidst the hay and some lengths of wood for a future barn. I had no idea what we were going to see; I just wanted to go somewhere.

The show was to be held on a farm six miles away, and the spring evening was warm as the cart made its way along the post road. Any form of travel was a balm to my soul, and I lay in the back looking up at the softening evening sky and wished I were on my way to some glorious battle or sea voyage. The sky was a great ocean and the clouds were ships. I awoke from a shallow slumber as the wagon rocked to an abrupt halt and we were stopped in a field, among many others.

The seats were already filling in the tent. Duncan and Robert and the girls found four together near the rear, and I was left to locate an orphaned perch for myself. This turned out to be good luck, as I made my way to the front and found a narrow spot on a bench between two corpulent farmers, only one row away from the stage platform. I can recall as if I were there now the shadows on the inside of the tent, the smell of bodies and the earth on which the benches were set.

At length, a man went around and dimmed the lamps at the perimeter of the tent, and then turned up the lamps along the front of the stage platform so that they cast light there, and the audience grew quieter.

A figure emerged from behind the canvas curtain at the rear of the stage, the footlights casting his looming shadow in triplicate on the canvas behind him. He seemed at least eight feet tall, an effect heightened by his satin trousers, which had vertical stripes that ran from his waist to his cuffs and glistened in the light, and a top hat that had met with some accident and was cocked in mid-rise. His shirt, also of some bright satin stuff, had puffy sleeves that billowed and swung when he gestured. His face was black, black as tar, making his eyes and mouth stand out in an uncannily exaggerated manner so that he resembled either a personable devil or a threatening angel. And he carried a musical instrument I had not seen before. It had strings, and the body was round, resembling a drum head.

This was Joel Walker Sweeney, a figure of legend now but at the time a mysterious apparition portending one knew not what. I believed him to be an actual Negro, and I gazed at him in awe.

Stepping to the front of the stage and grinning like a demon, he shouted, "*Good ebening, good ebening, everybody!*" and began playing his banjo. It was a jumping, twitchy tune—in fact it was no tune at all, but only a series of repeated rhythmic arabesques. As he played, he made some introductory remarks, quite at his leisure and unrelated to what his banjo was doing.

"*I hopes you is fine dis ebening,*" he said, as the banjo spun out its commentary beneath his voice. His dialect was strange and jarring to the ear—English, certainly, yet some rogue variant that forced one to pay attention in order to discern the sense. "*I has come from Old Virginny, a far piece for sho'. I got on board a locomotive, but dey had only built three mile of track so it didn't take me very far. Den I climbed on a packet boat on de Chesapeake, but don't you know dat boat sank. I swam ashore and found me an old mule to ride, but after a ways that mule took sick and died, and so I walked the rest of de way and here I is. At least I kep' my banjer wit' me and I may as well play a few songs for you good people tonight.*"

How to convey the atmosphere that settled over the tent? The swish his satin sleeves emitted as he switched and swung along the stage, the way his movements were timed and echoed the phrases of his songs and the banjo . . . He played at least six songs solo—I remember "Lucy Long," "Jump Jim Crow," and "Jim Along Josey"—before being joined by another fellow who played the bones and danced a marvelous jig dance. The songs beguiled me; they were full of improbable characters, tragic courtships, bullfrogs dressed like soldiers, talking birds. The sound of the banjo—part drum, part lute—set up an irresistible forward momentum, yet it constantly subverted expectation. Where you were led to expect a note, there would be an emphatic absence; where you had been led to expect rest, you would be pushed forward into the next episode. The banjo constantly insisted: "*And, and, and, and, and . . .*" Always more to come, never the possibility foreclosed, except playfully. I went into a kind of trance, as if he had cast a spell upon me . . . the shadows behind him, the proximity of all the other souls, the warmth of the evening . . . I was transported, lifted above the world and its tedium, as if a curtain had been pulled back and I had been told that all glory could be mine.

He played for what seemed both an eternity and the most fleeting of moments. During a spell of especially riotous applause, Sweeney left the stage, and I sensed a shift of some sort in the audience response. I returned to myself and looked around and realized that the performance was, in fact, concluded. People were getting up from their seats and making their way outside. We were being evicted from the circle of wonder and possibility and herded back into the lockstep of ordinary time.

In a kind of panic, forgetting about my brothers, and their consorts, and the entire material world for that matter, I struggled out from between the two profuse farmers, who were still whistling and bouncing in their places, made my way to the tent's edge, and slipped through one of the seams and out under the dark sky. My thought was to run to the rear and find this genius and say . . . I knew not what. But at the least I needed to know that this was not some dream I had conjured, that what I had seen existed in fact.

I ran alongside the tent as the applause abated, ducking the rope stays, and it was not long before I saw a flap which I took, correctly, to be the rear entrance to the stage. I carefully pulled it to one side, and there inside I saw the magic figure, sans top hat now, and another—the one who had done the jig dance. The great man was laughing over something, and he held a rag in his hand, and as I watched he passed it over his face and a large patch of his cheek changed color. He appeared to be wiping the very color off his face. After several swipes I realized that this was in fact a white man who had for some reason blackened himself for the performance. I was astonished. As he wiped, he spoke to the other.

"You came out of that turnaround very handily," he said. "I thought we were going to have to begin again, but you saved the day."

"Yes, well," the other said, wiping off his own face, "next time give me some signal that you're going to switch the rhythm. I nearly broke my neck trying to follow that."

"Don't give me orders, you sodomite," the tall man said, grinning genially and wiping off the last of the blacking. "I am captain of this ship."

"You are a freak and nothing more, a half-human fit for a circus freak tent"—the genius laughed at this—"half man and half jackass . . ."

"Only half jackass!" the genius said. "You have the full pedigree. Did you see the tart in the blue frock, by the way?"

"It's why I'm making haste."

I was shocked to hear them speak in this manner. I listened until, ambushed by the dust in the air, I sneezed violently. On the instant they both saw me, and the tall one focused on me, and our eyes met. I was no longer looking at an Ethiopian apparition, but at a white man, still in outlandish garb, and I thought he regarded me tenderly for a moment. The other watched both of us. I thought the tall one was about to speak to me; perhaps he would invite me in, take me away with them to wherever people did the things they did. He was half-smiling at me, steadily, as he reached over to a table, picked up something and, with a hard flick of his wrist, threw it at me. I ducked out of the way under the tent flap just in time to hear the object strike the canvas with a thud.

As if the devil himself were on my tail, I ran as quickly as I could around the tent toward where the last of the audience was leaving. My brother Duncan swatted me on the side of the head for giving them a scare that I had gotten lost, and they threw me in the back of the cart for the long, dark ride home.

From that point forward I was all but useless at the farm. I was convinced that some mistake had been made in the world's scheme, as if bills of lading had been mixed up and an order meant for one place had been set down in another. There was a world of color and song and movement, and it was elsewhere. I despised the routine, despised being at the mercy of my brothers' moods and orders. Count these and stack them and then count them again. All I could think of was escape.

Then one day, perhaps six months later, perhaps a year, a circus came through, set up very nearby, and stayed for a week. One could hear the riotous goings-on from half a mile away. They had contortionists and strong men and women aerialists and beribboned horses and a tired zebra. There was a small brass band ensemble and, very importantly, a performer on the banjo, Corbett by name, who blacked his face and sang while he played. There were also a number of sweepers and riggers and gatekeepers and such, and when the entire encampment departed on the eighth day, I was among their number.

I was berthed, with a few clothes I had tied up in a table-cloth, on a small, filthy blanket in the back of a wagon. As we pulled away and the farm slowly faded from my view I experienced a slight, fleeting pang of doubt, which disappeared when I felt a tap on my shoulder and turned to see another young circus hand offering me some peanuts from a bag. I never looked back again.

The work was not all that different from my duties at the farm, at least at first, but there was the immense advantage of a regular change in scenery. And stimulating company, with interesting stories to tell. Everyone did a number of jobs in the circus, even the performers, and we rarely had a moment of unoccupied time. Yet there was a feeling of freedom.

We proceeded through Pittsburgh, through Ohio, up to Cleveland, followed the lake's edge to Erie, then to Buffalo. We saw Rochester and Syracuse and Albany, by way of small towns like Auburn and Seneca Falls. Rivers, taverns, brown grass tramped down. Fires and the night and the morning's ashes. We set up our tents and wagons in fields near Pittsfield and Burlington and Portsmouth, and down again through Wilmington and across to Harrisburg. If any member of my family came to any of our performances in that area of Pennsylvania I would not know. By that time I had changed my name from MacDougall to Douglass, partly in order to save them embarrassment and also partly to betoken my new identity—I hesitate to say my "rebirth."

But in a sense that is what it was. One stepped through a portal into an alternate world when one took up with the circus, or any traveling band. The traveling world is parallel to the world of those rooted to one spot; it is the other end of the telescope, so to speak. Things that are taken by most people to have solidity and permanence become relative and subject to time. The church spire, the town hall or courthouse that watches over your days and is an ever-fixed mark to the merchant or the laborer, is to the traveling man only one among many such. The cherished touchstones of your daily life are to him a set of fresh opportunities for passing adventure, a source of profit to be extracted quickly, like gold from a small mountain, before moving on to the next El Dorado.

"Do you remember the set-to in the saloon in Pittsburgh? Where Halsey nearly got his eye put out by the drayman?"

"That was in Cincinnati. I know because I spent two nights with the redhead Jane."

"You may think she was a redhead but I saw her black roots!"

"I say it was Pittsburgh!"

"Nothing compares with the brawl in Ithaca."

"This we can agree upon."

. . . and so forth.

My three and a half years with Kimball's Circus were my Harvard University. I learned geography, history, economics, and no small measure of practical philosophy. I learned the ways of varied men and women, took informal seminars in music, physics, and animal husbandry. I acquired books in towns and read as much as time allowed. I was able to keep only a very few, as my berth in the caravan was tight indeed. I learned to coexist with others while asking nothing of them except that they perform their duties and allow me to perform mine.

And I learned the banjo from Corbett, or Brother Sam as he called himself when behind the burnt cork mask. He was in no way the equal of Sweeney in either virtuosity or personality, but he was someone to study. He taught me the secrets of the masquerade, the songs, the best proportion of grease to burnt cork. I also learned to manipulate the bones satisfactorily. He was the banjo player, and there could not happily be two in a troupe—and anyway there was only one banjo—so I learned the clackety-clacks, as one of my fellow riggers called them.

One of the great benefits of traveling was the opportunity to hear this or that local musician at his instrument, especially the Colored players. Set up in a boggy field north of Camden or west of Easton, and the sound of a fiddle playing an unusual variation on some familiar jig or reel would carry across half a mile from a porch or a stillhouse. If time allowed, one would visit with the fiddler, or the banjo player, exchange a tune or three, add to one's store of technique and repertoire. I was always struck by how welcoming the Negroes were, how willing to share their knowledge with us. They had no reason to be so. They certainly received no share of the profit we gained from their generosity.

Corbett was a genial, expansive soul, an adequate performer, and a fine raconteur up to the midpoint of whatever bottle he was emptying. But he was a hopeless drunkard, and somewhere around Hagerstown he was jettisoned, with regrets, in favor of one John Mulligan, about whom I must now speak.

Mulligan was ten years older than myself and had clearly served his own apprenticeship among the Colored players. He was an absolutely remarkable banjo player. Corbett had a limited repertoire, which he delivered competently, and with which he was content. But Mulligan was a fire-eater; his appetite for new songs, technical refinement, practice, was huge, as was his appetite for food. He was not nearly so girthy then as he later allowed himself to become. Mulligan was a large man in all senses, and deadly serious about playing the banjo. He had his eyes set on a musical ideal.

My first encounter with him was not promising. Although I was well seasoned after three years with Kimball's, I was not yet eighteen years of age, and when I suggested, shortly after his arrival, that the two of us rehearse a few songs together he merely grunted.

"Why don't you get me some water, boy," he said. "I am putting my banjer in tune." He was sitting on a stool in one of the tents, like a giant toad on a small mushroom.

"Why don't you get your own water," I said. "The exercise will do you some good."

This got his attention, and he stopped tuning and regarded me, for a moment, with a fierce expression, which almost immediately gave way to laughter—at my cheekiness, I suppose. I must have been a very unthreatening sight, myself, skinny as I was then, and standing with my bones at the ready.

"Let's see what you can do, then," he said, and without preamble launched headlong into "Buckley's Hornpipe." I was on top of it in no time and followed the tune's tricky switchbacks and crooked repetitions with ease. On the third time through I executed a few dance steps as well, while playing, and I saw Mulligan note them with surprise and approval.

When we had finished he avoided my eyes, but I saw him making some private adjustments in his assessment of me. Yet his first words were, "Now get me that water."

My response was a familiar obscenity, and I left him to find his own water. He never made the request again. And we were thenceforth on a much friendlier footing.

I was in earnest about performing, by that time. The homelier aspects of the circus life—the animals, the mud, the lifting and pulling—had begun to lose their charm for me, and it was music that offered a path outward and upward. Negro minstrelsy had become a national sensation. The practice of "blacking up" had spread from Sweeney and a handful of others to feed a hunger that had gone unrecognized until then. In it, we—everyone, it seemed—encountered a freedom that could be found there and there only. As if day-to-day life were a dull slog under gray skies, and the minstrels launched one into the empyrean blue. Even the sad songs—here was the mystery—were enlivening. We had heard jigs, we had heard ballads, we knew polkas and reels. But these Negro songs combined pathos and grandeur in the same taste; gaiety and tragedy wore not separate masks but the same mask. The arrangements compelled your feet to move, lifted you. Nothing like it had been heard in the history of the world.

Bands of four and five men—white men, of course—sprang up like wildflowers, holding forth from proper stages in real theaters in cities, and were attracting large audiences and large financial reward. The first of these bands that I saw was the Virginia Minstrels, so-called, with Emmett, Whitlock, Brower, and Pelham, in New York City. I went to see their performance at the old Bowery Theater, and I will never forget it. This was not just a man, however skilled, singing a few tunes, but a coherent musical group, with assigned parts, worked-out routines, harmonies. They exploded onto the stage; their movements, wild yet precise and timed to one another, expanded upon the music they made—tambourine, fiddle, bones, banjo. All were expert singers and dancers as well as masters of their instruments. Their performance galvanized me, as it plainly did everyone within hearing, and I resolved to form a troupe of my own.

Mulligan, it turned out, had been at the same performance, as well as several others by the same ensemble, at which he carefully studied the technique of the great Whitlock. When he and I met we were both carrying the same idea firmly—to establish a troupe—and after our initial skirmish we set to practicing with a singleness of purpose that was energizing to say the least. Our performances—Mulligan on the banjo and myself on the bones—began to be a primary attraction for Kimball, and it caused no small jealousy among the other acts, and at length we made up our minds to leave the circus at the end of a run in Camden and hop across the river to plant our flag in Philadelphia.

Mulligan had begun to defer to me in matters of business and organization. He was a great musician, but that is all he was. All his prodigious energies went into the subtleties of performance on the banjo. He was hopeless with money, and it was on this score, in fact, that I finally cemented an understanding with him.

Each week, Mulligan would no sooner draw his salary than it would evaporate like the morning dew in the harsh sunlight of a card game. He was forever borrowing money and sliding further into debt.

"John," I said to him one day after listening to his chronic financial lament, "have you ever thought to save your money?" Saving money was a skill I had somehow inherited from my Scots forebears.

"James," he said, "I cannot make ends meet as things stand now. How would I find two pennies extra, let alone enough to call 'savings'?"

"Let me do this," I said. "Have Kimball pay both our salaries to me, and then I will pay you myself. And after one month we will see if that works to your satisfaction. I will save your money for you."

He watched my face as if I had posed a very difficult mathematics problem and he was considering whether to attempt an answer. Finally, he said, "You would pay me?"

"Yes," I said. "And you may abandon the arrangement at any time you wish, and retrieve your escrows from me."

"Escrows?"

"Savings." He regarded me with a puzzled, vaguely suspicious expression, and I said, "John, you know where I am twenty-four hours a day. I could hardly slip out on you even if I wanted to."

Still somewhat puzzled, he agreed to the arrangement. He was making, at that time, twelve dollars per week; I was drawing ten. Kimball, after making sure that Mulligan was in agreement, began paying the full twenty-two dollars to me on every Friday, and I would pay Mulligan ten directly. He bristled initially, but agreed to see if he could live within the constraint. After the second week it began to seem normal to him. After the third I believe he forgot the arrangement entirely. At the end of the sixth week, when I paid him his Friday salary, I presented him with an additional twelve dollars.

Dumbfounded, he asked, "What is this for? Where did you get this?"

"These are your savings," I said. "You may collect them now, or I can continue to hold them for you and add to them each week."

His gaze bounced several times between the banknotes and my own face. He shook his head once, then again, then said, simply, "Thank you. Let's continue."

From then on I was treasurer of a corporation of two. And when at length we were ready to leave Kimball and make a start in Philadelphia, Mulligan ceded the helm to me in all logistical matters. Our reputation preceded us, and by putting out word that we were forming a troupe we quickly attracted interest from local players. This is how we found Powell, Eagan, and Richards, who was later replaced by Burke.

We put to good use what we had learned from Emmett and Whitlock, from Sweeney, and from the Colored amateurs we had studied and emulated. When we hit the stage there was no going back, for anyone. The curtain would rise upon us, seated in front of our painted plantation backdrop, and with a whack on the tambourine and my call of *"Good ebening, brudders and sistuhs!"* the hall was transfigured. We did not yet understand the nature of the illusion, nor that all the gaiety existed exactly because of the tragedy and injustice that even then bore down upon our nation. We would learn. But we did not know it then. When this elbow jabbed at the tambourine's thump, and Eagan's feet tapped out a tattoo as he played an Irish jig with an Ethiopian accent while Mulligan's banjo kept up a constant commentary, now mocking, now assenting, and my bones rolled chittering challenges at the others . . . well, the audience was transported, and we were as well. Even when Burke would arise to deliver a recitation concerning the demise of Old Master, or of a favored hunting dog, the presence of the black mask insulated us, and our listeners, from a full encounter with tragedy. It was our escape from our own yoke. It brought us alive.

Thus, the Virginia Harmonists. None of us, to be sure, had ever lived in Virginia. Yet we enacted our imagined scenes of plantation life, our comic dialogues, our walk-arounds and our solo routines, our "Boatman Dance" and "Clare de Kitchen," assuming a set of alternate identities behind the burnt cork, and we found a freedom there, behind the dark mask. The bitter irony of it all was as yet invisible to us. We were innocents, and yet we were complicit in a monstrous evil, in ways we could not see. But I am getting ahead of my story.

3

For six months, we performed at the Walnut Street Theater for a percentage of the entry receipts. "Theater" was something of a euphemism—it was really a wooden barn, which eventually burned to the ground, taking half a city block with it. Then Barton opened his theater on Arch Street; our reputation was becoming firm, and he hired us for a week's run, which became a two-weeks' run, and then we became a fixture.

Philadelphia was my Promised Land. The traveling life provided a sense of the new as long as you kept moving, as if you walked on water. Stop for a moment and you sank. But the city, at least at first, kept one afloat on a fizzing bath of stimulation and possibility. There was a great university, situated next to the lowest kind of taverns. Leafy, shaded sidewalks ran alongside fine wrought-iron fences, then gave way on the very next block to a series of dilapidated shacks sagging under a withering sun. If one walked two blocks one might as well have been in a different city. Dust and ceaseless noise behind makeshift plank fences, covered with handbills and posters, behind which buildings rose and fell. Citizens only two years removed from changing wagon wheels in the mud promenaded now in fine carriages. On the sidewalks one bumped into, or steered around, clerks, ministers, lamp-makers, thieves, professors, and prostitutes. One rubbed shoulders with more people in an hour than one might have met in a year in the country, yet the streets afforded a sense of privacy, almost of invisibility. People arrived constantly from points unknown and created entirely new identities for themselves, masks that hid their history.

Even our theater wore a mask. It announced itself to the street from behind grand Doric columns that rose two stories and supported a frieze with bas-reliefs of scenes from antiquity, and terra-cotta busts of Shakespeare and Marlowe, yet upon entry one attended animal shows, witnessed acrobatics and buffoonery of every type. And, finally and triumphantly, the performances of the Virginia Harmonists.

Mulligan and I selected the other members with an eye toward a balance of personalities that would provide variety and contrast. Powell was a simple fellow with a happy character; he had attended the university for one term and found himself unsuited for the academic life. I was perennially amused by his transformation into a tambourine-thumping whirligig onstage. Burke was our tragedian, master of monologues and tragic arias and hilarious anecdotes delivered with a doleful countenance. He set type for the *Clipper* in the small hours, after our show had finished for the night, and he was forever buttonholing me for advances on his weekly pay.

I never learned how he spent the extra money. Eagan, our fiddler, was handsome, thin, aloof, and mean. Of the members, he was the one with whom I felt the least affinity. Mulligan had pressed to include him on the basis of his instrumental finesse, which was unarguable.

Each had answered one of the advertisements we had placed, or had heard by word of mouth. Mulligan and I conferred on their respective musical and personal assets and deficits, and we agreed upon our final choices, but I handled all the details of salary, hiring, and conducting rehearsals to shape ourselves into a show troupe. All except Powell were older than myself, yet none seemed to bristle at my leadership, except for Eagan, who had an unerring nose for the exception to almost any judgment I would make. But generally, and certainly during our first two years, the troupe was harmonious in all ways.

On a typical evening, we would arrive at the theater around six o'clock to start preparing for our seven-o'clock show. I would arrive first, light the dressing room lamps, make sure costumes were in order. One by one, the men would straggle in. As if we were all waking up slowly, there would be muttered greetings, a general air of preoccupation, perhaps a small detonation of jovial abuse now and again, as we began the evening's transformation.

"Long night, Burke?"

"I fell asleep at the letter box and awoke with the letter 'E' embossed in multiple upon my cheek."

"Kolb's has added a bean pot at no charge starting at four in the afternoon." This was a favorite tavern, just across from the theater.

"Something to soak up the brew."

"Mulligan, is that a beard you're raising or has your jaw grown mold?"

Tuning his banjo, Mulligan impassively replied, "The greasepaint will cover it."

Eagan always entered looking the most dapper of us all and set purposefully to prepare himself for the evening, perhaps asking something on the order of, "Douglass, are we keeping 'Boatman' at the top of the second half? Have you determined?"

Slowly our street clothes were supplanted by our costumes. We had made the transition from the harlequinade of the earlier performers to full evening dress, but each with some exaggerated comic element—an outsized collar, mismatched cummerbund trailing behind, trousers cut three inches short to reveal red stockings. As we donned the stage garb we slowly joined our stage selves, discussing some bit of stage business that needed tightening or slight variation, mentioning the previous night's performance, sharing this or that story.

But the application of the burnt cork effected the true transformation, as if a lid were being lifted from a sarcophagus and some slumbering spirit were raised from the underworld. Each of us seemed to contain some other being who was allowed to emerge only once the face had been blackened. We would regard one another as if encountering our true souls, kept under wraps during daylight hours.

"*Good evening, Brudder Neckbones,*" Mr. Powell would say, applying finishing touches in the glass.

"*My finest elucimidations to you on this fine ebening, Brudder Pork Chops,*" I would reply. "*And Brother Scamp,*" I might say to Eagan, *"has you made de acquaintance of Bullfrog Johnson?"* At this, Mulligan, fully Bullfrogged, would imitate a croak on his fourth string, his face still impassive, and Eagan would produce a small, mocking glissando on his violin in response.

Slowly but inexorably, whatever cares we had brought into the room were replaced by a shared joke, a sense of having been freed. We had found the land of Eternal Youth. For a description of our performances from the other side of the proscenium, I can offer this brief sketch, from the *Clipper*:

> Several troupes in our City offer Plantation scenes and Darky songs, but the Virginia Harmonists are unquestionably the finest delineators of Ethiopian melodies and Terpischorean twists of a sable hue. They take the stage as the Greeks took Troy, with the audience their captives and conspirators. Mr. Douglass, as Brother Neckbones, is a most able and genial master of the revels, as well as a commanding manipulator of the bones. For 'Bullfrog Johnson' (John Mulligan), no praise will suffice; the equal if not the better of any banjo artist . . . His feature on 'Fire Down Below,' in which he nearly turns himself inside out, is astonishing. Mr. Eagan, on violin, provided the 'Old Virginia Reel,' during which time Mr. Powell on the tambourine composed a symphony of effects, as well as executing a fine 'backstep.' And Mr. Burke, as Brother Rastus, was most effective in his long monologue 'Massa's Last Farewell,' which left not a dry eye in the theater . . .

For nearly two years we were the acme of entertainment in Philadelphia. We even spent a month touring England, being toasted everywhere we went, and returned to find ourselves billed as "International Sensations." Our return was celebrated in the Philadelphia papers, and at least three other new troupes were doing all they could to eclipse our success. I took rooms in a good neighborhood, with a fireplace mantel of which I was very proud. I purchased two small framed watercolors for my parlor, and a set of fine silver candlesticks for my mantel, which set me back half a week's pay. I had finally climbed under the tent flap and into the magical illusion I had witnessed eight years earlier, when Sweeney took the stage in that nighttime field. I was a full-time changeling, a minstrel.

I was still a young man, barely twenty-one, yet I was able to assume an air of authority that was, perhaps, a kind of protective coloration. Privately, I had not finished being a boy. Some part of me remained one, even as I issued orders to my seniors. Famous behind a mask onstage, I walked the streets unrecognized by daylight, as if I were living in exile. It made me restless.

The world was restless, too. Two years into our tenure, competition from other troupes was beginning to siphon off the public's fickle curiosities. There were by then between ten and fifteen minstrel troupes in Philadelphia alone, not counting traveling troupes that came to town, and slowly they began adding other kinds of attractions to their bills in order to set themselves apart. First Laughlin, on Market Street, added an operatic specialty. Then there were the Swiss bell ringers at Sanford's, and an illusionist from Austria. Troupes were adding animals, female impersonators, elaborate costumes . . . The entire enterprise was beginning to change character, subsuming the mysterious energy of the pure Colored band into a broader entertainment. The Negro melodies and routines were still the heart of things, but set into a program that surrounded them, rather than comprising the entire world. As manager I had to take these developments into account, yet my heart was not in them.

Where once our house was packed every night, with almost no effort, now it required a stream of novelties to keep us between two-thirds and three-quarters filled on the weekends. I don't know that any other troupe was doing appreciably better, but the competition was spurring everyone to greater lengths. The first element I added beyond our core ensemble performance was a pastoral scene in which Powell and Burke portrayed Little Eva and Uncle Tom, in a tableau which I adapted from *Uncle Tom's Cabin*. Dramatized performances of passages from this book were almost a necessity at that time, and I worked up a scene in which pathos was ascendant. It ended with Burke on one knee singing "Ave Maria." Really, the effect was uncanny.

The new set pieces and routines demanded sufficient attention that we hired a costumer half-time, named Rose, to help us keep up with the various changes. I suppose this is the place to introduce her, but I hardly know how to begin.

She appeared at Barton's around the time I speak of and offered her services as a seamstress. She was tall, even in the flat shoes she wore, and her brown hair was cut short, so that it nearly resembled a boy's. Her eyes were large and brown. Her stated experience seemed in order with our needs, although I would have hired her if her experience had consisted of sweeping out coal dust in a bordello. I installed her in a large storage room that I cleared out immediately, and she was at work within a week.

I conferred with her on every detail of costuming. Every day she herself looked different, and yet every day her appearance bore the unmistakable impress of who she was. No one else dressed like her, walked like her. One day she wore men's trousers and a man's shirt, and she never looked lovelier. She called me "Mister James," with a little glint in her eye, for the first week, until I insisted upon her dropping the "mister." Her voice had a teasing lilt to it, but never cruel, and her natural state was an unhurried grace, as if she were the exiled queen of some unknown country.

At the sewing table she was as serious as a surgeon, and a wizard at finding ways to use unanticipated materials. I might stop in to find that she had managed to incorporate thin strips of foil into a set of pantaloons (for a Shakespearean parody) so as to catch glints of light; another time she created a pharaoh's headdress out of a frame of baling wire, covered with dyed muslin. She seemed utterly self-contained when she practiced her craft. I have always been susceptible to this quality in people, as I lack it myself. Part of me is always standing outside, weighing the costs.

We flirted good-naturedly—she flirted good-naturedly with everyone. On the days when her hours at the worktable overlapped with the troupe's rehearsals, she joined easily in the give-and-take with the fellows. Dan Powell might say, "Here is our beautiful flower! Remove your weeds so that we can enjoy your beauty!"

"You'd cut your fingers on my thorns, Dan," she might reply, with a smile.

Fitting Burke into an evening gown for some forgotten mock-opera sequence, she might smile to herself at a few words of praise from his middle-aged lips, respond, "I'm very flattered," without looking up, and thereby draw her boundaries in the gentlest manner. Only Eagan refrained from joining in the general teasing, and this should have told me what I needed to know.

One afternoon, a month or so after she arrived, I asked if she might join me for a walk and lunch at McKenna's place on Third Street. It was one of the few public houses that allowed women to come and go, catering, as it did, to travelers from the packet boats. She put some things in order at her worktable, and we walked the few blocks to the tavern. I was a bit on edge, as if I were about to submit to an important audition. I had to remind myself that I was the leader of a famous troupe, and not a schoolboy. I had had girls before—the circus made that inevitable—but I was unhorsed by Rose.

We took seats at a table by the window. The offerings were listed on a chalkboard on a wall. We read them.

I was tongue-tied at first, but I discoursed on upcoming routines and costumes, fearing all the while that her attention was only polite. In fact it was heroic, as I am sure I was boring her as much as I was boring myself. Somewhat desperately, I offered my anecdote about meeting Mulligan in the circus, his attempt to conscript me as his water boy, and finally she laughed. One wanted to earn those laughs from her. The mood between us warmed a bit. Finally it occurred to me to ask her about herself, and her own history.

It was clear, instantly, that this was a mistake. A pained look, and a retreat—momentary, but final.

"I'm sorry," I said. "Please, if that was intrusive . . ."

She regarded me with the queerest expression, searching my eyes as if to discover any ill intent. I had steered us onto a submerged reef, and I was at a loss for a correction.

At length she said, "You know, James, that I am spoken for."

"No," I said. "I did not know. I'm sorry if I made you uncomfortable . . ."

"No, you didn't," she said. "You didn't." She looked down at the table, where she worried a crumb with a lovely finger. "The world has not used me kindly."

If she had more to tell me, she kept it to herself. Behind her beautiful façade, apparently, lay some landscape of pain she chose to keep private. She trusted me sufficiently to let me know that it existed, yet I also understood that our relations would remain on a professional footing thenceforth. I wondered who the fortunate fellow was who had spoken for her, and how he had earned his position.

The answer arrived one afternoon, perhaps a month later. Dan Powell made some innocuous remark about Rose before a performance, and Eagan shot back, "That'll be enough of that." He had, we learned through his remarks here and there, installed her in her own apartment, which he referred to as a "bird's nest." A gilded cage was more like it, especially as he had a wife elsewhere. Whom we never saw.

In any case, I had more than enough to preoccupy me then. The fact was that our troupe's financial situation had become increasingly precarious, and things had approached the point at which our very existence could be in jeopardy if we did not find some way of attracting larger numbers. I kept this from the others to the extent that I could. But no matter how many birdcall impersonators, or jugglers, or Shakespearean parodies, we added, our receipts continued to fall steadily. I walked the streets, my head full of attendance figures and strategies for promotion, possibilities for new sketches, a thousand details, all the while feeling that I was missing something that lacked a name. We needed something to set us apart, again—to reclaim the public's full attention. I dreamed of Sweeney, of the elusive magic. I kept thinking that we needed something closer to the root of what had started us in the first place, the mystery in the tent, the dark outside, the shadows, the sense of something Other that was invisible by the light of normal daytime. And it was at that time that I first saw Henry Sims on the street corner.

He disappeared, that afternoon, as described, but he lodged in my mind. In those few minutes he summoned up for me the same sense of joy mixed with pathos, of humor, and of possibility, that I had felt seeing Sweeney in the tent. Yet here was no impersonation, no masquerade—he was the thing itself. I did not know his name then, nor anything about him. But it struck me that if there were some way of presenting him in the show, he might add exactly the element that was being diluted. The possibility of a kind of fruitful competition between him and Mulligan, orchestrated for maximum effect, offered itself. My imagining collected around him—a solo performer, as Sweeney had been, yet far more skilled.

There was one drawback, of course. He was a Negro.

Negroes did not appear onstage at that time, unless perhaps at some abolitionist meeting. To have a Negro appearing with a white troupe was unheard of—for that matter, against the law. Presenting him could easily get us closed down. One would have to think of some subterfuge, if one were even to attempt it in the first place. There was also the question of my partner, who was nothing if not proud of his own abilities on the banjo. In any case, before any of that, I would need to find him again.

I finally saw him some weeks later, playing outside the Black Horse Tavern. A crowd spilled out from under the awning that overhung the sidewalk, and two boys had climbed into the branches of an oak tree in the little park across the street in order to have a view. I was determined not to let my attention be distracted, even if a building were to collapse behind me. This time I would talk to him.

I approached the crowd's edge and stood on my toes to see. He leaned against the wall in the shade and wore an expression of grave and comic unconcern as he played and sang.

Said the blackbird to the crane,
When do you think we'll have some rain?
The pond's so muddy and the creek's so dry,
Wasn't for the tadpole, we'd all die . . .

He ran through several songs—"Mary Blaine," "Dan Tucker," and one or two others from the familiar repertoire. His singing voice was better even than I remembered; it alighted on syllables and bent them downward as an ornament might bow a tree branch, and he endowed unexpected words with a sparkling glow. His banjo playing was full of trap doors and tunnels; it galloped, jumped and turned, stopped, and doubled back. He had a number of songs with lyrics I had never heard, which seemed to carry a veiled significance. One went:

> *My old mistress had a dog*
> *Blind as he could be.*
> *Every night around suppertime*
> *That old dog could see.*

> *My old mistress had a cow,*
> *I know the day she was born.*
> *Took that old jaybird thirteen years*
> *To fly from horn to horn.*

In between songs, tuning his banjo, he seemed to register my presence—fleeting, but I thought I saw him mark me. Was it possible that he remembered my face from the previous occasion? All the while, he kept up a line of patter full of teasing and possibility, personalities assumed for thirty seconds and abandoned for others.

"And now, a song from my native land—*Spain*." General hilarity as he looked around in feigned affront. "*Que paso?*" he exclaimed. "*Pues no encuentro la maquineta de todos los postales y cuatro ramitos enchiladas . . .*" and so on, a fusillade of iridescent gibberish, pidgin Spanish that sent the crowd, myself included, into spasms of laughter. Plucking the strings in a deliberate *habanera* rhythm, he commenced singing,

Soft o'er the fountain,
Ling'ring falls the Southern moon.
Far o'er the mountain
Breaks the day, too soon . . .

. . . and everyone quieted down, entered the dream of the far-off border town, the doomed romance.

It was extraordinary. At one point I had to shake my head and look down at the cobblestones, with their mottled gray surface, the stains from the wine-seller's, and scuff my shoe back and forth to remind myself that there was a physical world outside the imaginary one he was summoning.

He finished and announced that he would take up collection. I kept my eyes on him as I made my way through the other listeners. When I was near enough to be certain I would not lose track of him, I hung back and waited for the last of his subscribers to make their donations, and then I approached.

He was replacing his banjo in a canvas carrying sack as I drew near. I had the sense that he was aware of my hovering, although he gave no acknowledgment. Behind him, the outline of the bricks on the side of the Black Horse Tavern were visible through a freshly painted advertisement for Bigelow's Bitters, with its smiling monkey; I was aware of a cart passing behind me, the mule's hooves making a sound like Powell clopping his coconut shells. I waited for him to acknowledge me, but he didn't. Finally he hefted his banjo in its sack and turned as if to leave, and I called out, "Hello!"

At this, he stopped and turned to regard me. Although we were the same height and size, he gave the impression of looking at me from above. He said nothing.

"May I speak with you a moment?" I said.

"You are speaking," he said.

"Of course," I said. "But . . . please. May I buy you a pint, inside?"

"I'm comfortable here," he said. "What do you want?"

His face and the backs of his hands were the color of copper, and his eyes were green, with long lashes. With a little art, he might almost have been able to pass for a white man, a Spaniard, or certainly a Hindoo at the least. I introduced myself and rushed into a confused oration about my admiration for his skills. As I spoke he glanced past me, and around us, at the activity behind me on the street, then back at me. I watched him measure my mode and quality of dress, the degree of animation in my face, my way of placing myself, even, on the sidewalk, and I saw him come to the end of what he could discover, as I continued chattering about his banjo prowess and command as a performer. I had the distinct sense that I was quickly running through my allotment of his available attention.

When, finally, I remembered to mention that I was a founder of, and performer with, the Virginia Harmonists, he stepped into the middle of my words and said, "Are you from Virginia?"

"Well, no," I said. "It is only the name we chose." I noted some small but distinct retraction in him. "What, by the way, is your name?"

"Ham Peggotty," he said.

I gave an involuntary laugh at the absurdity of this. This was nobody's name. God only knew where he had picked that up. "That is not your name," I said.

"Is there anything else?" he said, as if to bring our interview to a conclusion.

"Well, yes," I said, feeling a bit impatient, now. I was, in fact, irritated. I had just strewn superlatives around him like rose petals, and he was being incourteous, to say the least. "I would like to talk to you about the possibility of incorporating you into our performance in some way."

Now it was his turn to register my absurdity. He smiled for the first time, but more in mockery than in mirth. Once again he glanced around the streets, quickly. "I am not disturbing the peace," he said. "I am a free man, and I will defend myself."

"What do you mean?" I said.

He began backing away, keeping me in view.

"Wait!" I said. "What is wrong with you? I have a proposition for you."

He stopped ten yards away, by the entrance to the alley behind the Black Horse. I watched him look down the alley and make some signal with his hand, nod, and then turn back to me.

"State it quickly," he said.

"I would like to find a way of using your talents in our show," I repeated. "We perform every night but Sunday at Barton's Minstrel Theater, on Arch Street. You can see for yourself if you don't believe me."

"I have seen the handbills."

"Well, then . . ."

"How do you propose to present me on a stage in Philadelphia? You would be shut down."

"I do not know yet."

He regarded me for a long moment, looked up and down the street again.

"What position do you play in the line?" he said.

"I am on the end, with the bones. I can also play the banjo and the tambourine. You would not want to hear me play the fiddle, I'll promise you that."

"Walk down there," he said, indicating a dock area on the river, a block and a half away. "I will follow you, and we can talk there. Don't turn around."

Half certain that he would take the opportunity to run away while my back was turned, but with little choice except to do as he directed, I began walking in the direction he indicated. He was as skittish as a bird on a low branch. I was of course aware that Negroes were often prey to unscrupulous schemes, and my proposition must have sounded unlikely to him, yet I would have thought my sincerity was evident.

I arrived at more or less the intended place and stood for a few moments looking at the river. Half a block away some dock boys were hefting boxes onto a flatboat. I heard no footsteps, received no signal, and finally I turned around to look up the street. He was nowhere in sight. Once again, he seemed to have vanished into the ether. Well, I thought, I was right about that surmise, at least.

I was about to leave when I saw a movement behind some crates half a block away, and he emerged, looking once more up toward the top of Chestnut Street.

He pointed to a low platform nearby as he approached, and said, "We can sit there."

"Is all this necessary?" I said, half amused and half annoyed. "Do I seem so threatening?"

He didn't answer; I saw that he was holding something in his hand, which he now held out to me. It was a set of bones. I took them from him, as he pulled something out of a trouser pocket, with a rustling of paper.

"I hope you don't mind if I eat," he said, unwrapping a bun. "Play something for me."

I remarked to myself that although I was the one with the famous troupe, the accolades, the theater, I had somehow found myself in the position of being auditioned by him.

Anchoring the slightly bent lengths of white bone—about the size and shape of the doctors' tongue depressor—in my right hand on either side of my middle finger, I began with the necessary abrupt twistings of my wrist to set up the rhythmic pattern of "De Boatman Dance." The bones' chattering mimicked the ornamentations and arabesques of a fiddle making its way through the melody. I played the three-part tune through twice as he munched on his bun, watching me and emitting a periodic "Huh" if he heard something worth grunting about. He finished the bun at about the same time as I completed my audition, and he wiped his mouth with evident satisfaction.

"You know," he said, extending his hand to reclaim the bones, "in the third part you can decorate the long notes this way." Taking the bones, he demonstrated an effect that with a minimum of apparent effort extracted multiple clacks for each turn of the hand. I watched closely but could not see how he did it. He slowed down to half speed and still I could not make it out. He was watching me, as I watched his hands.

Finished, he replaced the bones in a small pocket sewn onto the side of his banjo's sack. "What do you want with me?"

I outlined in general terms that which I had in mind, my feeling about all the extraneous elements that were being added to the central part of the minstrel show, which central part was the Negro dimension. Glass harmonica players, operatic pastiches . . . As I spoke I got more passionate. I told him about seeing Sweeney, and the other minstrels, the pioneers of blackface. I told him of the exhilaration of hearing the music, playing it, and, above all, the feeling of freedom that had come from blacking up. "When I first heard the minstrels," I said, "I felt as if I had been freed from a life of oppressive servitude."

I suppose I conceived that this was all a kind of tribute to him, and his race, yet he was watching me with a face that might have defined irony. I stopped speaking.

"Have I said something wrong?"

With a look half amused and half derisive, he said, "Your eloquence is admirable."

"Will you come to the theater some time and have a look? You can enter with me, and I can install you in the audience, and afterward perhaps we can work something up. You may have an idea and I may have one . . ."

"Do you propose to pay me?" he said.

"I will pay you out of my own pocket if need be." I watched him register this. "Will you come, then?"

He stood, hefted his banjo in its sack, and said, "I'll have to see if I'm free."

"Wait," I said. "Will you tell me your real name?"

"Henry Sims." He said this in his Spanish voice, so that his surname sounded like "seems."

"Where may I find you? Can we discuss this further . . ."

"You found me twice," he said. Then he walked away, leaving me puzzled, and with the distinct feeling that I might never see him again.

I made my way back to Barton's, where we were to hold an audition for a group of Alpine yodelers. I was disinclined to sit still for this performance, yet it was my responsibility, along with Mulligan, to conduct these auditions. Mulligan and I sat next to one another in the fifth row of the dark cavern of the hall as the troupe trouped onstage in their ludicrous outfits. The women as well as the men wore leggings apparently intended to make them resemble sheep, but which only made them appear ridiculously hirsute. Mulligan found this impossibly humorous, which was not common for him, and he began making remarks to me, sotto voce, as the troupe ran through their audition songs.

"They really ought to shave their legs," he said.

"Quiet," I said, sliding deeper into gloom.

"Really, it is a troupe of epicene centaurs," he said.

"Will you stop."

"I wonder if they are equally hairy on their arms. We ought to present them completely undressed."

I let this pass.

"Perhaps we could breed them and shear them for profit."

Onstage, the group was doing some kind of truncated Morris dance and slipping into an antiphonal falsetto that was beginning to strike me as absurd. Mulligan continued chipping away with his deprecatory epigrams, and the troupe dipped and stomped and yodeled, and I was overcome finally with an attack of giggles which I tried in every way to stifle, unsuccessfully. Hearing my cackling, the troupe stopped in mid-yodel, and Mulligan, who was himself laughing, hollered to them, "You're hired! Mr. Douglass will talk to you about specifics when you are in your street clothes." As they filed offstage, accompanied by my helpless laughter, Mulligan said to me, "We can insert them in the middle of the second half. They will be perfect."

When I had myself under control, I walked backstage in a lightened mood.

For whatever reason, that night's performance was stellar. We were, needless to say, never less than professional. Still, for the past months we had rarely been more than professional. Yet as any performer will tell you, once in a while something gets loose and, like birds gathered in a tree creating a racket, everyone is subject to the same mysterious visitation of energy. It was certainly so on this night. Our first half was robust if not epochal. After intermission, the Parakeet Impersonator (a German) whom we had added as that week's specialty was received respectfully, but then we took the stage and "Across the Sea" extended itself under our feet and fingers and we all seemed to levitate six inches off the boards, and I remember looking across at Mulligan and feeling the hair rise on my arms. During the final number, "Clare de Kitchen," Mulligan rose to his feet and squared off against Powell, and they jumped back and forth across the stage as if they were attached on strings to one another. Finally I rose to my feet as well and circled them, and Eagan—Eagan!—sank from his chair to his knees, playing variations I'd never heard before. Although the house was only half-full, I thought the audience would tear the theater down, and we had to play three encores.

And yet, when the performance was finished for the evening, all went home in different directions, and one was left alone, alone. Descending abruptly from the peak of performance, one returned to one's rooms, or to a tavern, to hear the chimes at midnight, or at three in the morning. It had been an extraordinary day, yet it was ending in a way that had become painfully familiar. Along the quiet street, through the gate which Mrs. Callahan locked at eight o'clock each night, down the quiet hallway, and into my parlor, where I shut my apartment door behind myself and lit the lamps. I was still a young man, I told myself. I sat on my divan and read for a while. And after a while I set the book down and went to bed. It was far better than carrying sacks of grain across a muddy field, as I had remarked many times. Yet it occurred to me to wonder, as I turned down the lamp on my nightstand, where Henry Sims was, and how he made his peace with the night.

4

It was springtime in Philadelphia, and my gloomy mood did not last. I got up early the next morning and walked through the bright, still-damp city, through the sidewalk tree shade along Sixth Street on my way to the theater. I thought I might show up early, take care of a few business matters. Three creditors were becoming insistent, and we had sufficient funds to satisfy only two of them. Birch and a crew were supposed to be building a small replica of a cabin, on rollers, as an enhancement to our Uncle Tom segment, and I needed to see how that was coming along, as well.

The theater was alive with hammering and shouts, all of which emanated from Birch and two assistants. I made my way to the stage and regarded what they had done, which was perfectly serviceable.

"We'll put a porch on it tomorrow," Birch said, wiping his face with a rag.

"Why does it need a porch?" I said.

"For Burke? Didn't you want him sitting out front?"

"I suppose," I said. "But won't that make it more difficult to maneuver on and off the stage?"

"We'll make it so that it's detachable."

I nodded, looked inside. "Put a chair or two in there, and maybe something on the walls," I said.

After they'd finished and Birch had left for the morning, I took lunch at Kolb's, directly across from the theater. I liked the heavy, stained-wood paneling in the place, the lingering smell of beer and sauerkraut. I had my own napkin, and my own stein, and the house cat, Abel, knew he could count on a scrap or two from my plate. I lingered a while over one of my notebooks to finish scratching out a few notes toward a routine I was developing. Afterward, on the sidewalk, I stopped to let my eyes adjust to the day's brightness. I looked across Arch Street at the façade of our theater—the stone steps, the two-story columns, the frieze above, with its lyre and laurel. A mockingbird had perched atop the bust of Shakespeare and sang in full voice. I've always loved those birds—the inexhaustible variation in their songs, the way they find the highest perch, the beautiful arrogance, the absolute freedom. I stood listening for a full minute, then I stepped off the curb, and as I did so I heard someone say my name. I turned, and there, in a doorway, stood Henry Sims. His banjo, in its bag, leaned against the door frame.

I was so surprised to see him that it took me a moment to locate words. "You're here," I said, finally and brilliantly.

"Can I see the theater?" he said. He wore spectacles now, and a brown plaid shirt and a pair of very fine hunting boots, which were utterly unfit both for the city and for the warm weather.

"Well," I said, "of course." We continued to stand regarding one another for a moment or two, and then he picked up the banjo in its bag and we started across the street. He was younger than I'd first taken him to be. We were, I realized, not far from the same age; perhaps he was two years my junior. As we crossed, his gaze scanned the street up and down.

"I'm glad you came," I said. "Have you been out performing?"

"No," he said. "I don't do it every day."

"Here," I said, "this way."

We entered the shaded alley that ran alongside the theater and continued down the cement walkway. I tried to arrange my thoughts as quickly as I could; this was the opportunity I had wanted, but it had arrived before I quite knew how I wished to handle it. We got to the stage door, which had been propped open. It was chilly inside, and we paused to let our eyes adjust to the relative darkness. There were always a few oil lamps set on a table by the door, and I located one and lit it, and we started walking through the curtained gloom of the backstage area.

"Watch for the ropes," I said. Our backstage was full of traps for the unwary or the uninitiated—coils of rope, stacked wood placed anywhere for convenience, wardrobe racks, parts of moving sets retracted into the wings and beyond. Henry stuck close to my right elbow as we made our way.

"Here we are," I said, opening the door into the dressing room, which was also still dark. I crossed to the dressing table and lit both lamps, and the room came into being.

"You can set the banjo down over there," I told him.

He looked around the room, and as he did, I followed his gaze to the large mirror which hung lengthwise on the wall facing the dressing table, with a diagonal crack and pictures affixed to it, a cloth flower pinned on one edge. The necessary materials arrayed on the table: jars, wigs, pencils. Leaning in the corner of the room was Jenny, our mascot, a carved and painted wooden figure of a woman—some lost boat's figurehead—gazing at the ceiling. Powell had done time as a seaman, and he brought her in for good luck. We were going to hang her over the dressing room door but we hadn't got around to it. Someone had placed a straw hat on her head. A steamer trunk in the other corner, a low divan, and a large closet, the doors open, hooks on the doors hung with braces, vests, shoes arrayed along the bottom. Scattered around, and piled behind the divan, were props abandoned by visiting acts—three Indian clubs left by a pair of Chinese jugglers, a birdcage with a shoe in it, several coils of rope to be used with a trapeze assembly, a string of paper-cutout silhouettes.

"It's quite a circus, isn't it?" I said.

"When I got to Philadelphia I thought the theaters only had Shakespeare plays. Maybe operas."

I was surprised to hear Shakespeare's name from a Negro's mouth. I wondered where he had picked that up. "How long have you been here?" I asked.

"A while," he said.

He examined some of the jars and bottles, and he picked up one of the salvers of burnt cork mixture. He rubbed a bit of the sooty mess between his fingers and thumb, took some and smeared it across the back of his left hand. He stared at it.

"It's mixed with a bit of grease so that it won't sweat off easily," I said.

"I had an idea about how you could present me."

"Did you?" I said, slightly taken aback. As I faced him, I realized that the frames of his spectacles were empty of glass. He saw me notice this, and a slight smile shifted his features. I started to say something, and then I decided to hold off. This, I thought, is a fellow who likes to raise questions. "Let me show you the stage, and then we can talk about it."

A sharp, narrow vein of light divided the heavy maroon draperies, which stretched far up into the darkness overhead. I pulled the curtain to one side and we stepped out onto the wooden boards of the stage, lit only by two lamps mounted on the side walls. Birch had left them on when he had retired for the day. I pointed to a row of metal shells with gas spigots inside, set along the stage's edge. "Later, all those will be lit, and you see the reflectors that illuminate us." Beyond the edge, the hall, still dark, yawned like the mouth of Jonah's whale.

Looming over the stage from behind was our elaborately painted backdrop depicting a plantation scene—an elegant mansion house surrounded by magnolia trees, among which gowned women and waistcoated gentlemen watched with benign amusement as a few typical Darkies danced a jig. We had three different backdrops that we used to great effect during the performance, but this was a masterpiece. Henry stood for some moments, regarding the scene with interest. As he did so, an utterly unexpected embarrassment began to rise in me. I wasn't sure why; the figures were, after all, strictly a comic convention, and a universally employed one, at that. Still, I steered his attention elsewhere.

"We set up here," I said. "Our chairs in a crescent like this. We step forward in turn, here, for solo pieces—songs, dances, banjo specialties, what have you . . ." I stopped, then said, "You're all right, are you?"

"Yes," he said. He walked to the edge of the stage, looked out into the shadowed cavern, up, around. He turned back to the plantation backdrop again, took in the entire stage. He walked to stage left, then back across to stage right. His manner was that of a landlord, surveying a new property holding. His footfalls echoed in the empty house. As if registering this last fact, he executed a quick dance step on the boards at the front of the stage, and the pattern rippled through the hall like wavelets on a pond.

We returned to the dressing room; Henry sat on the divan next to his banjo in its sack, and I sat at the makeup table. I found myself fidgeting with a grease pencil, and I set it back down.

"Well," I said, "is it what you expected?"

"It's big," he said. "How many people come to the shows?"

"The hall seats eight hundred."

"Tickets are fifteen cents?"

"Yes they are," I said, surprised that he had checked independently. "Let me tell you my idea of how to present you," I went on. "Then you can tell me yours."

I had come up with the notion of stationing him behind a large sheet, with lights in back of him projecting his shadow forward, so that the audience would see a dancing, outsized silhouette. This had a certain novelty value, and it answered one obvious challenge, although it left a number of others un-addressed. Still, I thought it was rather ingenious.

When I had outlined the idea, he gestured dismissively and said, "Why don't I put on the greasepaint with the rest of you?"

"The greasepaint," I said. This stopped me for a moment. He was already a Negro, if a fairly light-skinned one. Why would he need to apply the cork?

"You can't present me as I am," he said.

"No," I said. "I cannot."

"Right," he said. "Well, the audience would think I was one of you."

"One of us," I said. "You mean a white man."

"Yes," he said. "Pretending to be what I am."

Now I saw what he meant. A kind of double masquerade. It was an audacious proposition, even an elegant solution. Yet, as I mulled it, I felt uneasy. There was something very intimate about the transformation we underwent in the Virginia Harmonists. Whatever our individual differences, the assuming of the burnt-cork mask amounted to membership in a kind of brotherhood, or even a mystery cult, minus only the Masonic trappings. I felt oddly exposed by the idea of a Negro joining us in the ritual.

"My mother," Henry continued, "told me, 'If you want to hide something, leave it where everyone can see it.'"

Then he stood up and walked to the dressing table, touched the burnt-cork with one finger and, looking in the glass, painted a mustache on his upper lip with two quick swipes. Stepping back and regarding himself in the mirror, he laughed at his own reflection.

* * *

It was well into the afternoon, and I did not want to take more chance than I already had of his being discovered at the theater. I told him I would consider his idea, and if I could find a way of executing it soundly, we might give it a try. I told him I would need to discuss it with my partner. I gave him the address of, and directions to, my apartment, and we arranged to meet there in two days, after I'd had a chance to bring up the idea with Mulligan.

Before he left, he asked me about payment. I had anticipated this, in fact, and had given it a bit of thought. I was certain he could not have been making more than two dollars per day, playing on the street, based on what I had seen. The members of the Virginia Harmonists were paid quite well. Powell and Burke each drew sixty dollars per week, Eagan sixty-five, at his heated insistence. Mulligan, as cofounder and lead soloist, drew seventy-five, and as manager, and everything else, I took eighty. We earned substantially more when we traveled, although there were overhead expenses involved. Based on what I estimated that Henry earned, I offered to pay him four dollars for a night's appearance with us. This money would come out of my own draw, as I did not want to ask the others to subsidize the experiment, at least not initially.

When I named the figure, he looked affronted, repeated the words "Four dollars?" and fixed me with a disappointed frown.

"Well," I said, aware that it was a slightly low figure, "how much did you expect me to offer?"

"I won't appear for less than ten dollars." He gazed at me through his glassless spectacles.

"Ten dollars!" I said. This was outrageous, although I had to admire his cheek. That was nearly what Mulligan made for a night. "In no way will I pay you that kind of money. I will pay you five dollars and fifty cents, and no more than that, for one show only. If that show goes well—as I expect it to, mind you—and we feature you regularly, we can set a figure with which we are both pleased."

He looked down at his banjo in its bag, nodded as he picked it up, and said, "That will be fine." He stood up and shook my hand with a formality that was almost comic. I had the sense that he felt he had done well for himself. He said he would look forward to our meeting in two days, and then he left.

After he'd gone, my mind was awash with questions, all amounting to one question: Now what? How, really, could we present him onstage, given his race, without inviting trouble? If we did proceed, how to ensure that his secret would not somehow be found out? And how, indeed, could I introduce the idea to the others, and especially to Mulligan? Importing the fellow into the act, in whatever form, would upset a balance we had achieved through long practice and, eventually, habit.

There was the question of how to convince Mulligan to take a chance on a Negro performer. I knew that he was as discomfited by the parade of silly side acts as I was. Yet it would be difficult enough to sell him on the idea of adding another banjo player without handing him this very reasonable objection with which to kill the idea in its cradle. I thought that if I could secure a hearing for Henry, at least, then we could settle the details afterward. His presence and virtuosity would make the case for him.

There was another question, as well, that lurked underneath these. My years in the circus had trained me not to press an individual about his background—one's talent and willingness to work were one's passport. But this was not the circus. I was the proprietor, and I had the welfare of the troupe and its members' livelihoods to answer for. I knew nothing at all about the fellow, except that he was a masterful musician and performer. And I was not sure that I wanted to know more. There was certainly the possibility that he was a criminal, or a runaway. Yet it was unlikely that a criminal or runaway would present himself for daily public scrutiny on the streets, much less on the stage of a theater. There was something about him that did not conform to any template I had encountered. But by the time these thoughts had formed themselves, I had already determined to stow them. We needed something new, and this would be something new. It involved a risk I felt we needed to run.

I wrestled with the question of how to tell Mulligan, and I wrestled more, and finally I decided not to tell him at all. I decided that I would introduce Henry to the troupe as a Mexican. His skin was light enough for this to be plausible. I had heard Henry do his pidgin Spanish voice, which I thought was good enough to fool anyone who didn't speak the language. I doubted that Mulligan, or anyone else in the troupe, knew Spanish. I would say that I had heard him playing on the street—that much was true enough—and had managed to convey to him my interest through sign language and a few Spanish phrases I had picked up in the circus.

It was an outlandish story, admittedly. But there was no question about our increasingly desperate situation as a troupe; Henry, in whatever guise, would inject new and necessary energy into our presentation and, I would gamble, attract fresh customers. I had no doubt that he would know what to do on a stage. I envisioned him in the old-style Sweeney type of costume—a phantasm of the earlier type of minstrel—a brilliant rustic among the mock sophisticates. If we could settle on the best way of introducing him, and then turn him loose, I was sure that he would be a sensation. And if we maintained the fiction that he was Mexican, then we could, if worse came to worst, claim ignorance that he was a Negro. We could remand him to the fates, if it came to that.

Armed with my provisional plan, I took Mulligan aside during the next afternoon's specialty audition—dog tricks, this time. A half-dozen terriers, arrayed in a line, trained to bark out the rhythm of a handful of songs—"Old Folks at Home," "Oh, Susannah," and some others, disfigured more or less beyond recognition.

"Why do we need him?" was Mulligan's first, and understandable, response when I presented the idea to him.

"We need something," I said. "We need to set ourselves apart again. We are sinking. How many yodelers and bird trainers can we present?" I looked up at the stage, where Birch was cleaning up after a mess one of the dogs had bestowed upon our boards. "Or dog acts."

"And why won't he do a formal audition?"

"He is very shy, and embarrassed about his bad English. And anyway, he has auditioned for me, in effect. I'll vouch for him."

"And he will black up?"

"To be sure," I said, keeping my face as blank as possible.

"And one song only?"

"Correct."

Mulligan, watching my reactions, frowned and said, "Why the mystery, James?"

"I can't tell you more. I have reasons."

I watched him weigh the costs and benefits of pressing the point. "How would we introduce him?"

"I would think in the second half . . ."

"Of course."

" . . . he could wander onstage while we were doing patter between tunes. Or I could be introducing Burke's monologue. He could walk on, looking lost and mystified."

Mulligan nodded. "And one of us will say, *'Why Brudder Neckbones, who's dat nigger poking around in our yard?'* "

"Exactly," I said.

" *'Maybe he's dat chicken thief dey told us about, come from de next plantation!'* "

"Yes," I said. "General consternation, protests, mayhem."

"That's good," Mulligan said. He emitted a short bark of a laugh, envisioning it. I was pleased to see him warming to the scenario so quickly. Then his face clouded over.

"What's wrong?" I said. But I knew. "John, this fellow is no Mulligan. The rest of the line can say, *'Bullfrog, is you gonna take dat sittin' down? Show him!'* And then you wash away the memory of him. Yes?"

"And afterward, something on the order of, *'Nobody beats Bullfrog!'* I must prevail."

"Little question of that," I said.

"We'll need to rehearse this," he said.

This was impossible to do without Henry's identity being revealed. "I would prefer not to," I said.

Mulligan watched me, silently. At length he said, in a calm voice, "James. What are you about, here? Is he a criminal? What is the idea?"

"He is no criminal," I said, remembering that I had no idea if this were true. "Please trust me. We can give the boys the scenario in general terms; we can improvise dialogue on the spot. There are reasons for keeping it a surprise." I looked hard at him. "Everyone will benefit. If it does not work out, we have the opera singer on tap, don't we? What was her name?"

"Gloria."

"Gloria," I repeated. "My God, do you remember Fatima, from Kimball's?"

"Fatima?" he said, as if I had just awakened him. "Fatima . . . Oh God, of course. I still . . ." He shook his head.

"Let's keep our spirit of adventure alive, shall we?"

He nodded, looked as if he were about to speak. At that moment, Birch interrupted us and the discussion was tabled, but I took it as a tacit assent.

I was elated. But, like a splinter just beneath the surface, something nagged at me. I was now keeping a secret from my closest associate and, in truth, the only person I could remotely call a friend. I was discovering a vein of recklessness in myself that quite surprised me, as if an entirely different person were inside, using me as a disguise. It was not an altogether unpleasant sensation. But it was disquieting, as if a lost relative had shown up with a dubious proposition. We were up against it, was what I told myself.

* * *

On the appointed day, Henry showed up at my apartments, his straw hat replaced by a woolen slouch cap pulled low over his eyebrows, which he kept on after he was inside, until I reminded him to remove it.

"Welcome," I said.

"Good," he said, looking around the room somewhat nervously. "Thank you."

"Would you like some lemonade?" I said. Mrs. Callahan had prepared some and kept it in a shared icebox.

He raised his eyebrows and nodded his head, and I left the room to get us a couple of glasses. When I returned with the glasses of lemonade, he was standing in the same place where I'd left him, still holding his banjo in its bag. I told him to set the banjo down and have a seat on the divan.

Gradually he relaxed enough to maintain his side of a modest volley of conversation. He asked if I owned the house where we were, and I told him that I only rented it. He wanted to know if I had lived there for a long time, and I told him it had been about three years.

He had plainly been raised well. He had, in fact, an air of affronted nobility, which both attracted me and aroused a certain resistance. He was at no great pains to please. As we made small talk he emitted amusing sayings. Unsure whether he had heard some remark I had made, I repeated myself, and he said, "I heard you twice the first time." At one juncture I asked if he had ever seen Sweeney perform—I was trying to find out where he had acquired his prodigious repertoire—and he responded, "We went to different schools together." I never did determine where he had picked up his repertoire.

When it was time to start playing music, we sat facing one another on two straight chairs. As we got ourselves arranged, he became completely focused on the task. I brought out both my pairs of bones, one pair for each hand, and waited for his banjo to meet his strict requirements. I had the sense that the building could have been destroyed by an earthquake while he tuned, and it would not have made any difference to him.

Hearing him play on the street was thrilling, but actually playing with him was an experience of another order entirely. He knew all the songs that were standard fare for the minstrels, and dozens—perhaps many dozens—more. From the beginning of any song he would add tiny elements, grace notes, instant echoes of some errant accent I played upon the bones. He had a manifest horror of repeating himself, and any given song would change aspect constantly as it went along, while yet remaining recognizable. He brought out an adventurous spirit in me, and I would try to match him arabesque for arabesque, turn for turn. He played with his eyes closed much of the time, except when our ideas for variation would meet in an especially felicitous manner, and then he would look at me and nod. I think it is safe to say that I had never felt such a combination of concentration and freedom.

When we had finished an invigorating run-through of "Mary Blaine," I said, "Well, that could not be improved upon." He frowned and played a small figure, something he must have thought he had played imperfectly, for he repeated it with slight variations of inflection, accent, intonation, at least twenty-five times before he called a provisional truce with the troublesome phrase. He might, I thought, have been more of a perfectionist than Mulligan.

We played for well over two hours without a rest; the sunlight had stolen across my parlor floor without my noticing. We took an intermission, then, and sat drinking the last of the lemonade.

"Well," I said, "I spoke with my partner, and I think we will go ahead with things."

He slapped his knee in triumph.

"But there are some wrinkles."

"What wrinkles?"

"I determined that it might not be best to tell him, or the others, straight off that you are a Negro."

He nodded, waited for me to go on. Then he asked, "How did you plan to hide that?"

"Yes," I said. I felt as if I were about to leap from a tall perch into a very small pool of water. Nothing for it but to jump. "I told him that you're a Mexican."

He looked at me as if I were joking.

"I have heard you speak Spanish, on the street . . ."

"But . . ." he began, then he stopped, squinted at me. "I wasn't speaking real Spanish."

"I know that. Listen," I said, "this is merely to get your foot in the door. I don't want to start by encountering some resistance that we could easily avoid."

We went back and forth about it and slowly teased out the rest of the plan. In addition to presenting him to the others as a Mexican—named "Juan García"—we determined that as an extra element of disguise he would meet them already blacked up. We encountered only one major impasse in the original plan: he did not like the idea of stepping onstage for one song and then leaving, as Mulligan and I had discussed. I told him that one song was the limit of what Mulligan would agree to. After some argument, he suggested that he be onstage from the beginning of the second half, seated until "noticed" and called upon to prove his prowess. As a refinement, we established that he would be mute the entire time. In tribute to his nonverbal eloquence we would call him Demosthenes Jones.

Was this entire idea brazen, and perhaps unhinged? Yes. Yes it was. But suddenly the predictable continuum of the everyday was replaced by a set of effervescent possibilities, and that, I suppose, was what I had been addicted to my entire life. The process was intoxicating, as music was. It was all just plausible enough to seem workable and practical. And what, I asked myself, was the worst that could happen?

Letting Rose in on Henry's identity was unavoidable; he needed to be fitted for his outfit, so there was no way around it. Or perhaps it was in fact avoidable, yet I needed to share the secret of my plan with someone, and the idea of a complicity with Rose was too attractive to deny. Of course it was a risk, yet I had a strong intuitive notion that it would be all right, and that she could be trusted with the secret. By this time, Rose and I had become . . . not friends, exactly, but we had a certain comfort with each other that comes from understanding that neither person's boundaries would be tested further. Still, I thought to check with her first on the question.

"Rose," I said, "we are going to need an outfit for a guest performer, but his identity needs to be kept secret. Even from the fellows."

"All right, James," she said, stitching carefully.

"Listen, Rose," I said. "I need to be certain that you will keep the secret."

She looked up at me for a moment as if to see whether I were joking. "Do you imagine I can't keep a secret?"

"Well . . ." I began.

"I would win medals at it, if they awarded them," she said. Then she added, "You would be my only serious competition."

"Then I'll ask you this: Do you have antipathies toward Chinamen, Negroes, Mexicans, or other foreigners?"

Now she looked hard at me. "I take people as I find them, James." Her look of reproach made me confident that I could import Henry without causing uneasiness in her.

Two days later, in the late morning, Henry met me at the theater so that Rose could take his measurements and get to work making a costume. She was wearing a simple frock, and she had on a washwoman's bandanna, tied around her head. But this touch had the paradoxical effect of making her seem even more elegant than usual.

"I bought some embossed satin for the costume," she said. "The receipt's on your desk. I'm going to make a turban with the leftovers. Maybe you'll let me play an Arab princess."

"I'll conduct the audition privately," I said, flirting back with her.

"You'd like that, wouldn't you?" she said.

"Well," I said, "why don't we get Henry fitted?"

Henry was standing back in the shadows; I turned and threw him a quizzical look. He stepped forward, and I said, "This is Henry. But we are going to do a little routine for the boys, so think of him, for now, as Juan."

He stood there, wordless, with his hands in his trouser pockets. Rose was frowning. I worried that I might have misjudged Rose's willingness to accept a Negro, but the worry passed when she spoke.

"Aren't you hot in that flannel?" she said.

"No," he said. "I'm fine. It's chilly in here."

"Is it?" she said.

There ensued an awkward silence, which I broke by suggesting that we get Henry measured, and we proceeded to Rose's workroom.

Once there, Henry submitted to the usual measurements. Rose showed me the bolt of glossy light-green satin, embossed with shiny stripes, which I agreed would be perfect.

"Well," she said, "what kind of routine are you preparing?"

I explained about the Spanish masquerade, and she laughed.

"Do you speak Spanish?" she asked Henry.

"Not really," he said. "Just a type of joke Spanish."

"He sounds absolutely like a Mexican," I said.

"Let me hear!"

Henry let out a sentence, something on the order of "*Dos manicómios de jueves éstaban ricos con la segura . . .*" with a kind of insouciant authority that would have been quite convincing to anyone who did not know Spanish.

"What did he say?" Rose asked, turning to me as if Henry would not understand the question.

"He said, '*The sky turns red when the turnips are in the basement.*'"

Henry laughed at this, and so did Rose.

"Close enough?" I said.

"Close enough," he said.

We discussed a few more details of the costume, and Rose

was all business. At the end of our discussion she wished us good luck with our routine and said the costume would be ready in a few days, as soon as she got the Uncle Tom suit altered for Powell. This was fine, as we were just shy of two weeks away from Henry's debut.

Henry and I quit the theater. I had errands to run, and we walked a ways together along Arch Street. Henry asked me for Rose's name, and I told him.

"Didn't I introduce you?" I asked.

He told me I hadn't, and he added that he had never seen a woman with hair that short before.

"Yes," I said. "She's unlike anyone else."

"Is she your sweetheart?"

He wore a slight smile as he asked this. I did not know whether to laugh out loud or to cuff him. It was not the kind of question one asked. And it touched a sore spot in me, of course.

"No," I said, rather curtly. "She is kept by one of the troupe. Eagan."

"What do you mean, 'kept'?"

"I mean," I said, "maintained. Paid for, housed, clothed, and whatever else you might imagine, in exchange for his pleasure."

This came out more harshly than I had intended, although it was certainly the truth. I glanced at Henry and saw an expression of gloom settle over his features, a brooding look, almost angry. I thought that he must be quite an innocent to have had no experience or awareness of such an arrangement. Our paths diverged at the next corner, and Henry mumbled his goodbye and walked off under a cloud, carrying his banjo.

I let the others know that we would be adding an extra attraction for one number in the second part, on Saturday two weekends hence. There was curiosity and more or less happy acceptance from Powell and Burke; as they never heard the other acts in advance, they were satisfied to accept my brief précis of the situation. Mulligan, of course, had already been apprised, and he kept his own counsel, although I sensed from his facial expression that his misgivings had had time to breed and perhaps ferment in the days since our conversation. Eagan on the other hand, would not let it alone.

"I had the idea that this troupe was a collaborative venture," he said.

"What makes you doubt it, Michael?" I said.

"Some of us are now privy to a mystery, for which the troupe as a whole is footing the bill. And a Mexican, in the bargain. Who is this fellow, anyway? I suppose the troupes of Austrians were not enough. At least they are white men."

"I am paying for this out of my personal receipts, Eagan," I said. "So you needn't worry about the impact on our finances. And in what way does his color weigh on the discussion, Brother Scamp?"

This question stopped him momentarily, although he recovered himself enough to mutter, "I don't care for intrigue."

It was only with the greatest effort that I was able to restrain myself from mentioning his own arrangement with Rose in this connection, but I did restrain myself, and the matter of Juan García was allowed to rest, for the moment, without further discussion.

And I waited for the day to arrive, full of anticipation. So much depended upon the success of our scheme. I knew nothing about Henry, really, nor did he appear to care who I was or where I had come from. The point of our intersection, the plan we had improvised, the music we made, was what mattered. How lucky we were, I thought, to have the theater. What would any of us do if we did not have these roles to play? If you could truly see into the face in the mirror . . . well, who among us would willingly do that? And if we knew who stood next to us at the market, or who passed us on the street, who sat beside us in the theater, if every grave could speak, as in the old ballads, we might not be able to bear living. We never do truly know what others think. And may it please God they never learn what is in our own black hearts.

PART II

5

In the still of the day the horse carried him slowly along the graded path under the elms, past the quarters toward the mansion house. Dragonflies hovered and zagged in the shimmering heat. The few slaves he passed averted their gaze. The rifle in the hide sheath; the turned, whitish eye. Nobody could have mistaken him for good luck.

He had been summoned and had come in his own good time. Stephens he knew by reputation, as he knew most of the planters in the area. A drunk with pretensions, a notorious libertine with a big library of books, so he'd heard. And a succession of slave mistresses whom he kept like wives until he tired of them and turned them out, either for sale or to the fields. Nothing very unusual about that, except for the artifice of keeping them dressed well and living in the house. Tull had heard that Stephens had taught two of them to read. Or had someone teach them. The real wife, the white one, had died some years back.

The man's house boy had been gone five months. Stephens placed newspaper advertisements, had handbills printed and posted both locally in Virginia and in Northern cities, increased his reward offer, all to no avail. And had finally sent a message to him, enlisting his aid. It was, he would have been the first to admit, a last resort. Not only because of the expense—a daily allowance in addition to travel funds and incidentals, along with the reward money itself—but because of who and what he was. No respectable person would have much to do with Tull Burton. Especially not a lace-curtain bitch like this James Stephens.

Stories about Burton were his calling cards. Three years earlier, a strong and unbroken slave named Silas had run off from Fontainebleau Plantation, twenty miles to the south, and was rumored to be hiding in a swampy tract of woods another ten miles out. The plantation overseer would not go after him, and the master, a fop in green velvet, had sent for Burton. With two accomplices and two dogs, Tull had tracked the runaway into the deep woods and found him in a tree, from which he refused to descend.

Tull had been through it before, and he always felt anger at the runaways' refusal to acknowledge the nature of the situation, at the waste of time and energy, the forestalling of the inevitable. It was an overcast day, chilly and disagreeable to begin with.

"Come on down, Silas," Tull said. "You're going home one way or another."

"I don't have to talk to you," the runaway said.

"You're going to suffer more than you need to," Tull said. "Get down now."

"Shit on your mother, drunk."

Tull nodded. To one of his men he said, "Start a fire over there," indicating a spot ten yards away. The man handed his dog's leash to the other assistant and went to gather some sticks.

"I don't drink, Silas," Tull said, pulling his rifle out of the sheath that hung alongside his saddle.

"I don't have to talk to no white man," the runaway hollered, his voice on the edge of hysteria. "I'm going to Cleveland, or either Mexico . . ."

To his second man, Tull said, "Tie the dogs to the wagon and get ready to grab him." The other had gotten the fire started.

"I'm not working no more, and I'm not getting whipped, and your mama likes when I stick it in . . ."

Aiming for the runaway's shoulder, Tull fired one shot, which hit the mark and caused the slave to lose his purchase on one of the limbs to which he clung. Hanging on with his other arm, he struggled to get a leg up over the limb. Tull aimed again and fired, and this time after a brief and futile twist of his torso the slave fell to the ground, making a gurgling sound, an animal sound, angry, pig-eyed . . .

The two men lunged and grabbed him.

"Ohhh," he hollered. "White man died on the cross for me . . ."

Tull approached, bent down, and forced a dirty saddle rag into his mouth.

"See, nigger? You were right. You don't have to say a thing." Grunts, struggling. "Pull down those rags." The breeches, secured by a length of worn and greasy rope. The man who had built the fire got them undone and yanked them down, exposing the runaway's rubbery, flopping genitals. "You sure stink, nigger," Tull said. "You ought to take a bath." Tull pulled out his hunting knife and, saying only "Hold him," grabbed and stretched the penis and cut it off at the root. The runaway emitted a choked scream from behind the wadded rag in his mouth; his eyes rolled back in his head.

Tull tossed the wad of flesh onto the ground by the dogs then walked to the fire and held the tip of the knife blade in the flame for fifteen seconds, turning it on either side. He walked back and, saying "Hold him steady," cauterized the nub as the unfortunate man in his care writhed and twisted.

"Now see, nigger? I let you keep your balls. You like to talk so much, why don't you say thank you? My Mama is sure gonna miss that thing." Drawing back his boot, Tull kicked the writhing man as hard as he could in the side, driving it into the slave's lower ribs, and they all heard the snapping sound.

"Now put him on his stomach and get him tied," Tull said. "Throw him in the wagon when you got him right. I didn't finish my lunch."

The group arrived back at Fontainebleau late in the afternoon. As they approached the mansion house, Tull told one of the field hands watching the procession to run and get Master real quick. They pulled over by the stable area. Five minutes later, Master Arthur came sauntering down the path to where they were. He was well turned out—immaculate white breeches, a green velvet waistcoat, and a lace scarf at the neck, setting off his puffy pink face. Tull watched him with disgust.

"Yes," Master Arthur said. "I see you have brought me something." The slightly brusque heartiness masking a degree of impatience, or perhaps nervousness.

"Throw back that canvas, Olds," Tull said. The man did so, revealing the slave, with his rags down around his thighs, his midsection a mess of clotted blood. His head was near the foot of the wagon, between Tull and Master Arthur. One eye opened, slowly, in the Master's direction, unseeing, clouded. The Master gave a reflexive wince, an intake of breath, a slight frown.

"There's your man," Tull said.

Master Arthur regarded Tull now, with some mixture of shrewdness and fear. "Well," he said, "he's hardly any good to me in this condition, is he?"

The words "is he?" angered Tull—the easy superiority, the indifference to the suffering staring him blindly in the face. And trying to get out of paying, clearly.

"You said dead or alive."

"Well, he's not much of either," the Master said. A faint trace of a smile around the edges of the eyes. "Is he?"

Tull drew his pistol and with no further word forced the barrel into the runaway's mouth against the rag that was still there, pulled the trigger once and sent blood, brains, and the top of the runaway's skull spattering all over the Master's breeches and waistcoat. The saddle rag, still wedged in the slave's mouth, caught fire.

"Dear Christ," Master Arthur said. Steadying himself on the side of the cart, he bent over, retching.

Tull watched him for a moment. "Now," he said. "Are you going to pay me my money?"

This was a language everyone understood, and he was generally recognized as effective, ruthless, and fair. He was the hire of choice for the most challenging jobs. The masters were themselves afraid of him, but they knew where they stood at least. And beyond that, he expressed something inside them which they expended their resources in keeping disguised, even from themselves, and yet which was the foundation of their world. For his part, Tull took no pains to disguise his contempt for the planters' false aristocracy. He had no friends. He took pride in his work, he expected full and prompt payment, and otherwise he kept to himself. He was a professional.

He drew near the carriage entrance of The Tides now, and upon dismounting was received by a black gatekeeper, in livery. Gold epaulets, fancy stitching, dirty collar and knee stockings. Buckled shoes. A type he hated; it made Tull sick. This footman had a fringe of white hair around his bald scalp, bulging eyes, and a goiter under his left ear.

Without making eye contact, the servant took the reins and said, "Master James Stephens will see you in the parlor."

"Really?" Tull said. A smile slowly disfigured his face, like blood seeping through a bandage.

"Yes, sah." No eye contact.

"Take good care of my horse, now, Sambo." Fixing him with his stare, willing the old man to look at him.

"Yes, sah." Still the unconcern, tying the reins around a post. "I'm called Atticus, sah."

"Tell your mama I said hello, Atticus," Tull said, starting toward the door.

"Mama in a better place," the servant said, under his breath, as Tull walked away.

An older woman servant greeted him at the door and walked him down a short hallway to the main foyer, and through that to the parlor. The plaster had fallen away from a part of one wall in the foyer, and there were gray smudge trails above the wall-mounted oil lamps, unlit, now, in the daylight. The parlor itself was large and bright, with windows stretching from the floor up to the picture-frame molding above. The sunlight had faded the upholstery on the furniture— velveteen settees, French chairs. Fissures in the plaster, here and there. The usual oil portraits on the walls; above the fireplace, a giant, thick, ornate gilt frame surrounded a large mirror, darkened by decades of fugitive smoke. Several large chips of gilt had gone missing from the mirror's frame and left irregular white patches among the baroque curlicues. A huge, faded Oriental carpet covered much of the floor.

The Master would make him wait; that was part of the transaction, always. Tull kept his hat on; it was made from a hide of some sort, of a peculiar dark brown color and texture. He remained standing. When the man finally entered— white hair, and a full head shorter than Tull, wearing a red cloth jacket—he dispensed with any greeting, saying, simply, "Please sit down," and indicating a blue brocade chair. He regarded Tull's hat, pointedly, but he did not ask him to remove it.

"You've read the note I sent," Stephens said, once they were seated.

Tull nodded.

"You must have questions you need to ask."

The man's hair, mostly white and yellowed, was swept back somewhat theatrically from his forehead. His eyes were green and he had long eyelashes that Tull thought looked like a girl's. Tull guessed that he had applied some rouge discreetly to his cheeks. He was skinny and slight but not muscular; a boy's body, with a paunch behind the embroidered white vest. He smelled of rosewater.

"Why did he run off? Did he get a beating?"

"I never beat him. He lived comfortably and never lacked for anything."

"This boy lived down in those quarters I passed?"

"No. He lived in a small house twenty yards off the kitchen, to the east."

"He had his own house?"

"He lived there with his mother and one brother."

"His mother is still there?"

"Yes."

"Is there a father around?"

The master looked at Tull for two full seconds before saying, "The father is unknown."

So, Tull thought. That was easy. Just to be sure, he smiled, nodded as if in accord, and said, "These nigger bitches can pick up extra weight anywhere, can't they?" He watched Stephens's face mottle with red, and then he knew for certain who the father was, and he saw that Stephens knew that he knew.

"Where do you think he went?" Tull asked. "Do you have any idea?"

An attractive slave girl in her teens entered the room carrying a tray with two glasses and a pitcher of lemonade. She stood in front of Stephens, seemingly unsure what to do. Tull watched Stephens avoid her eyes and say, "Thank you, Aurora." The girl frowned slightly as he took one of the glasses. "You may put the tray down on the table after serving Mister Burton." She approached Tull, who looked her directly in the eyes and gave her a big smile. She was very scared.

"You can just set the tray down right there," Tull said. "Thanks, Aurora." Her hands shook as she set the tray down and walked out of the room without a word.

"I am assuming that he has found his way to some Northern city."

"That takes in a lot of territory, Mister James. Any hints about which one?"

"The most likely are those I listed on the advertisement I included with my letter. You may call me Mister Stephens."

"Sure," Tull said, allowing himself a short laugh at his own expense. "Sorry to presume, Mister Stephens. You don't think he went to Canada?"

"No."

Tull studied the man's face. "Because the mother is still here?"

Stephens looked away and made an indefinite gesture, half raising a hand from the arm of the chair, shrugging.

"You said he played a banjar."

"Yes."

"Where'd he get it?"

"I always assumed that Enoch made it for him in the woodworking shop."

"Where's that?"

"I'll have Atticus show you."

"I want to talk to the mother, too."

Stephens nodded.

"That's all right with you?"

"Certainly."

"They were close?"

"Very."

"Anything else you can tell me?"

"He often performed for guests or entertainments. There's no doubt that he has the banjar and will find a way to perform somewhere."

"There's not a lot of places for niggers to perform, Mister Stephens."

"He is resourceful and intelligent and he will find a way to do what he wants to do."

"You liked this boy pretty well."

"He brightened many evenings here." Stephens looked as if he were going to add something, stopped, pursed his lips, and with a slight shake of his head let it go. He began to stand up, but Tull remained seated.

"We need to discuss terms."

"Yes, of course," Stephens said, sitting down again.

After laying out the terms—seven dollars per day plus expenses, plus three hundred dollars reward money, fifty of which was payable immediately and nonrefundable—Tull said, "I assume you want this boy brought back in good shape."

"I want him brought back. Alive if possible."

"If possible?"

"Correct."

"What if he doesn't want to come?" This was as close as he came to irony.

"I have made myself clear."

"Actually, Mister Stephens, not quite. You're telling me you want him dead if it comes to that."

"Yes." Now Stephens stood up, picked up a small bell from one of the end tables, and rang it. Within moments, Atticus appeared. "Atticus, please escort this man whither he asks." Then, to Tull, who was still absorbing surprise at Stephens's request: "An envelope containing your initial payment and an advance on expenses will be waiting for you when you are finished."

Tull nodded; no hand was proffered to shake, and he walked out of the parlor with Atticus, leaving his lemonade untouched.

The woodworking cabin was some hundred yards away from the main house, and Atticus walked Burton there without speaking. It was one of the larger dependencies on the grounds, well-tended, shaded by two large trees. Tull ordered Atticus to wait for him outside.

Inside, Tull found a tall Negro, built very solidly, wiping something off his hands with a rag.

"Your name is Enoch?"

"Yes it is," the slave named Enoch replied. "Sir."

No "yassuh" for this one, Tull thought. As his eyes adjusted he saw that the slave had features that were about half African and half white, despite his dark blue-black skin. Blue eyes, and intelligent. This was his little kingdom, Tull thought.

"I'd like to ask you a few questions, if I may," Tull said, all politeness. "If you have the time." This slave wore some kind of green and red scarf around his neck—silk, if he wasn't mistaken.

"I will answer if I can," Enoch replied. Well-spoken; he had learned manners somewhere, probably hired out to some city business for a year or two.

"May I sit down?"

"Please do," Enoch replied. "I hope you won't mind if I remain standing."

"Enoch," Tull said, "I don't mind if you take one of those rasps you got there and jam it into your ass and file yourself down to a pile of shit. Just answer my questions."

Enoch made his face a blank. "Yes, sir."

"You know this boy who ran off, Joseph. Master James says he used to spend a lot of time here. Is that right?"

"Yes, sir."

"What can you tell me about him. Start with how he looked."

"Joseph not a very handsome fellow, I would say," Enoch began. "Quite dark-complected, almost black as me." He gave out with a hearty, utterly false laugh that might have fooled some, but not so practiced an operator as Tull Burton. Nothing enraged Burton quite so much as for a slave to think he could fool him by assuming the same ingratiating mask that slaves habitually wore for their masters.

"Let me stop you right there, Enoch." Tull watched the smile remain on the face as the eyes grew masked and watchful. "You know who I am, and if you don't anyway you know what I'm here for. You know what I do. Is that right?"

"I have an idea of that, sir."

"Now when your master tells me that Joseph has light,

copper-colored skin, and you tell me he's black as you, who do you think I'm going to believe?"

"I does my best to be truthful, sir."

Tull nodded, looking at the man with something that could have been mistaken for tenderness. The "I does my best" was another mask. He was frightened.

"You see this hat I'm wearing, Enoch? Have you ever seen one like it?"

Now the slave was quiet and Tull could feel the fear coming off of him. He said, "No sir."

"That's because I made it myself. Cut the hide, cured the skin, shaped it and blocked it. Anything look familiar to you about this skin? It's got a nice color, doesn't it?"

Enoch stood motionless and silent.

"Now, I'm not playing around with you, Enoch. You answer my questions straight and I'll have no complaint with you. I don't want to hear another lie from you. We looking at the same horse, now?"

"Yes."

"Good. Now about how tall is he."

"He come up to about here on me."

Tull nodded. "All right. Would you say he was pretty smart?"

"Joseph smarter than everybody here put together."

Satisfied, now, Tull said, "He worked with you here in this shop?"

"Sometimes he did," Enoch said. "He was mainly what you call a house servant. He taken care of Master's clothes and such. He worked in the pantry seeing after things. But he liked to come down here and he liked for me to show him how things works."

"What about the banjo. You made him a banjo?"

"Yes, sir."

"You taught him how to play the banjo?"

"I showed him some little things on it, but he taken to it just like some people natchly know to ride a horse."

"What did this banjo look like?"

Enoch's eyes were closed, and Tull gave him a moment, then said, "Tell me what the banjo looked like."

"About like that one over there," Enoch said, opening his eyes and pointing to a corner of the shop. A crude instrument leaning up against a chair in the corner of the room.

"Get it and bring it here."

Enoch did so, standing in front of Tull and holding the banjo for inspection. The body was a small, hollow gourd with a side sliced off and a skin stretched over the open part, secured with small black nails. The neck seemed to have been part of a broom, or perhaps a shovel handle, sheared so that there was a flat surface for a fingerboard. Three strings ran the length, secured at the top by roughly cut wooden pegs attached to a flat piece through holes, as on a violin. Another peg, screwed to the side of the neck about halfway down toward the body, kept a short string in tension. Like the others, it ran down to a small wooden piece at the bottom, to which they were tied; they were held above the surface of the skin by another little wooden piece with notches to hold the strings in place. This little bridge was just below the center of the skin.

Tull tapped on the skin twice with his fingers; the head was taut. He reached and took the instrument out of the slave's hands and set it across his own lap. Enoch watched him. With the nail of his right index finger, Tull snapped down on a string; the sound was muted and died out very quickly. He snapped down again, twice, and plucked the short high string. Even in the small shop room it was a quiet sound. Tull played a little tune, a jig, thirty seconds at most, and then, finished, handed the banjo back to Enoch.

"Your master said Joseph played for dances."

"Yes, he was very good at playing for the dances."

"Nobody could hear this thing over a pair of shuffling feet, let alone a room full of dancers."

Enoch was quiet.

"What banjo would he play for dances?"

Enoch was quiet.

"The reason I'm asking, Enoch, is because Master said that Joseph lit out with a banjo you had made for him that he used to play for dances. He kept it in the house where he lived with his mother, and it was gone." A muscle in his neck was rigid. "Are you going to tell me the truth?"

"It was just like mine I got in back."

"Then let me see yours, Enoch." Staring at him.

The slave walked to the back of the room, twisted a small piece of wood that kept a door closed on a rude hutch, and pulled out something that looked more likely.

"Bring it here."

The slave handed Tull a larger instrument; the body had been made not from a gourd but from a grain sifter, a rigid wooden hoop. A larger skin had been stretched taut across it and held in place by a couple dozen tacks around the outside perimeter. The neck was a section of a table leg, planed down flat on one side to about a third of the original width, and left round underneath. It was a well-made instrument; the hoop was over a foot wide.

"You made this yourself?"

"Yes."

Along the rim Enoch had inlaid crude wood marquetry in a herringbone pattern. At the top, where the strings were attached—four, this time—the head had been inlaid with a harlequin pattern of marquetry, and on the back side of the head a man's face had been carved, quite skillfully, into the wood. Laid into the fingerboard itself, next to the side peg for the short string, was a tiny metal horseshoe, maybe half an inch long. Pewter, Tull thought, or maybe lead.

"Joseph can do this kind of work, too? He does woodworking?"

"Joseph can do a little. I taught him some."

Tull righted the instrument in his lap and played a bit, as he had played before. This time the sound was considerably louder and fuller. Tull stopped playing, stood up, and started for the door, carrying the banjo.

"Much obliged, Enoch," he said. "You can keep the other one." He stepped out through the door with the banjo and walked to where Atticus stood waiting under an oak tree.

"Come on, take me to the mother."

The house in question was compact but, again, nicely tended. Slightly larger than your normal run of cabins, even for favored house slaves. Raised two feet off the ground on piers.

Still, not all that much more than a shack, Tull thought. Some flowers planted out front, struggling.

"Wait here," Tull said.

Two wooden planks were steps up to the door. Tull opened the door without knocking.

The woman at the table, combing out some sort of yarn. At the unannounced entry, seeing the banjo in his hand, gasped. An expression, then, of dread, as if he were a poisonous snake.

Tull sized her up, figured her to be in her mid-thirties. She was still good-looking, but probably past her usefulness for the old drunk in the mansion. A boy maybe ten years old stood by a small stone fireplace where a fire was going despite the heat. She watched Tull with high alert and fear. She knew, he thought.

"You know what I'm here for."

"Coley go in the other room now."

Tull smiled at her, at the comedy of mistaken identity. "I'm not here on a buying trip, ma'am."

"Coley, you hear me."

The boy stepped backward into an adjacent room.

Tull saw her take in his hat, his turned eye. No; she knew.

"I think you got it figured out," he said.

She was silent; he could hear the doors being locked inside her. Battening down the hatches. The dread and fear joined now by an attempt to steel herself. Tull knew the routine, the familiar stops along the way.

"I don't want any unpleasantness," he said. "I want to know where your boy ran off to."

She sat staring at him.

"All right," he said. "I'll ask you one more time. Where'd your boy run off to? Your boy Joseph."

"You not going to find him," she said.

"I didn't ask you," Tull shouted, his face suddenly mottling red, "if you thought I would find him. I asked you where he ran off to." Tull saw her breathing a little faster, the face still impassive. He let himself settle for a moment, then he said, "Before I ask you a third time, you think about this. Joseph can come back, alive. He'll get a whipping, but it's not going to be too bad because his daddy loves him." He saw her frown; that was good. "And he'll be alive, and you will have your boy with you."

"He won't come back."

Tull leaned across the table and slapped her hard across the face with the flat of his hand. "You shut your fucking mouth unless you're going to tell me where he is." He didn't like getting angry; it was a loss of control, and the only antidote was to use it to dominate a situation absolutely. He felt himself getting sexually aroused—another way of losing control. It made him angrier, harder.

He stood up and walked around the table to where she was; with his right forearm he pushed her yarn and tools off the table. She got out of her chair, grabbling at the dowel stick for the yarn, and as he grabbed for her she caught him on the side of the head with it. It had no effect. She screamed, and as Tull jerked her bodice down, ripping the fabric, the boy Coley ran into the room, crying. Tull had his knife drawn and was holding the sharp edge against her nipple and she was weeping.

"Philadelphia," the boy yelled, crying and pushing at Tull's leg. "Joseph said he going to Philadelphia."

Tull looked at the boy, across the woman's body. He was holding her down by the neck, with the nipple still pinched between his thumb and the knife. He looked at the boy directly and calmly in the eye. "Are you telling the truth?"

"Leave Mama be. Joseph said he gone to Philadelphia and bring us there to be with him."

Tull kept his eyes locked into the boy's until the boy shut his eyes and collapsed in sobs. Leaning down now and looking directly in the woman's face, he said, "You raised that boy right." Then he squeezed her nipple, hard, between his thumb and the knife blade and cut off the tip and flicked it away. She called out to her God as Tull wiped the blood off his knife onto her dress and stood up.

"I think you're about finished nursing babies anyway," he said. "If I'm wrong at least you got one tit left."

He picked up the banjo from where he had leaned it against the wall and stepped out into the beautiful, hot afternoon.

6

Night. Not the barn, not the ravine, not the skiff tied in the rushes. He touched the wall. Somewhere outside, distant, a shrill voice arguing. All dark.

Henry slid his legs over the edge of the narrow pallet and put his feet against the floor, felt for the matches, lit one, and the small room bloomed dully with murky light and twitching shadows. Slowly, slowly, he rejoined himself, and his pulse settled, slowly. The tiny room in the entrails of Lombard Street, with its built-in drawers and cabinets—done by a riverboat man, so he'd been told.

He put the match to a candle stub in a low brass saucer, left there by someone, sometime. In the dark, the past stood on equal footing with the present. In the day the sun cast your shadow and you knew where you were. At night it was harder to tell, easier to slide backward.

He had had no particular plan beyond getting to a free state. They wanted him to go to Canada, but Philadelphia suited him. What they called Bottle Alley was an entire city block carved into a warren of rooms along a network of passageways off Lombard; Mr. Still's man Sam had told him about it after he had spent some weeks with the Passmores, way out on the Germantown Road. Staying at the Passmores' had been a temporary measure, arranged by the Vigilance Committee, while he got used to being free. They were good people and generous to open their home to him. Yet when he offered to play and sing for them on the second evening, Mistress Passmore put her hand on his arm and said, "Please . . . we can't have this here." They said it was a slave instrument, and he had thought, I am nobody's slave.

During those first weeks in Philadelphia, he had been taken to abolitionist meetings, usually at churches, where he felt himself on exhibit, like a circus oddity. The earnest white people pressed his hand and wished him Godspeed. He did not want to be ungrateful, but "Godspeed" sounded as if they wanted to get rid of him, fast. One Pastor Radford would introduce one Mr. Linforth, a Friend To The Bondsman, from Buffalo, New York. Mr. Linforth would intone: *"Brothers and sisters, how can we, as Christians, as men and women of good conscience, look the other way? Like Pontius Pilate, we find no wrong in the miserable wretches subjected to the daily Crucifixion of whippings, arbitrary separation from loved ones, and worse, much worse, and yet still we remand them to the whims of a murderous mob. Imagine yourself, unable to do the least thing without the imprimatur of a sinful human who crowns himself your Lord and Master. Imagine misery, unalleviated by the slightest glimmer of hope. Beauty, the joys of a family, the very basis of humanity a closed door to you, reduced to the level of animals by the inestimable cruelty of the lash and the branding iron . . ."*

Henry, or Joseph as he had been called, was not whipped. He had not worked in the fields, not slept on a mud floor, had not spent all day picking, lifting, carrying. He had, perhaps, a special perspective. But in his experience, even the lowest field Negroes at The Tides weren't animals and didn't think of themselves as animals. In fact they had a kind of contempt for Master James and the others of his class. To the abolitionists, Henry was a representative of a subjugated people, nothing less, and nothing more. It was his role. Certainly the idea that there was any fun to be had in the world seemed to be taken as an affront.

He reached for the banjo leaning in the corner, lifted it into his lap. Deep midnight, but day would come. Touch of the wood, the taut strings. Softly, he thumbed the lowest string, and it warmed the room. Thumbed the next string, then the two again, a note between, quiet so that only he could hear. Playing, he knew he was there; it put him in time, yet out of time, too, the pattern now buoying him like a tide, like a river, like the river . . .

Banks of the Rappahannock in the chirping noonday. Bulrushes, frogs. Those are boats that come and go.

Through the woodshop door the bright sun, and a juneybug crawling through the wood curls. Tiny blocks, sanded for no splinters. The horse was a horse. Enoch made the horse.

This is the Bible. These are words. God is a Word and He is all around. They lived in a garden and there were snakes down by north pasture. All the animals went on a boat when it rained. There was a frog in the puddle. Found him later dried and dead.

Plates go here. Napkin there. Knife and fork and spoon. Here is a cup; here is a glass. This is a broom. Sweep like this toward the middle of the floor. Like this.

The table set for dinner and a cloth that Mother sewed. Gold sun outside and tree shade at dinnertime and then He blocks the door. We about to eat. Joseph go outside go play. Go now. Later Mother did not talk.

This is how you hang Master's shirts. This is how he likes his tea. This is how you shine his boots. Always in a row like this. These are Master's breeches. That is Master's coal and that is Master's bucket and that is Master's fireplace and that is Master's table and those are Master's footsteps. Master likes his hoecakes nice and brown and why did Penelope laugh at that. Atticus didn't laugh. Marcellus brought the coal in.

In the Mansion House there was a room with books and he said, So many Bibles, and Mother said, No they are different. Each one is different. Every day was the same but every book was different. Every day they had the chores. It was better than the fields; he heard that more than once.

Enoch made a table, made a chair, made the shelves for Master's books. The table was from a tree. The wood comes from Richmond. This is maple, this is walnut, this is cherry, this is pine. This is hard, this is soft—look how you can do with your fingernail. Hold the rasp this-a-way. You see? Like this. Hold the saw like this. Cut away from your hand. Look how I learned that lesson. He held up his hand where one finger was gone.

Enoch made a wooden rose. Enoch made a horse and carriage. Enoch made a banza with a gourd and a goat skin. The strings were fishing line. Joseph made a table leg and

Enoch said that was good. You getting big enough to handle that saw.

The book was from a tree. Davey was a boy in a story and he loved his mother, and his father died and another man came to the house. Mistress taught Mama to read and Mama taught Joseph. Mistress hung herself over the barn rafters.

The world assembled itself slowly. He was twelve. Master James said he was getting tall. Put his hands in his hair and said, "Bushy, bushy," and laughed and laughed. Not too tall for me to go bushy bushy. "Irish eyes and Mandingo hair." Funniest damn thing ever. Joseph didn't see what was so damn funny. He learned to say damn from Cassius at the stable. Master's breath always smelled of the whiskey he drank. Joseph knew because he had tried it himself one time out of the glass decanter on the silver tray and he got sick and his mother said she would have whipped him but it looked like he didn't need a whipping, that whiskey had whipped him plenty.

Enoch was hired out to a man in Baltimore for a year. By then Joseph could do the necessary small repairs in the wood shop. Better than folding Master's shirts and shining Master's boots and hauling Master's damn coal and smelling Master's breath. He liked being alone in the shop, and now he had other things on his mind. Like watching Aurora switch under her skirt as she carried the milk from the dairy. He felt his blood burning him alive from the inside out. Was careless one day and damn near cut his little finger off, cut it almost to the bone. Mama put something on it made it sting worse than the cut and wrapped it up in gauze. Looked at him while she was wrapping. Something took your mind off what you were doing? Looked like she knew.

The boats went up and down, and he had a week to watch them while the hand healed. Everything was alive and everything spoke to him, and down by the river sometimes he would take care of himself in the rushes, and afterward he would watch the tow boats and the barges and the steamers and wonder what they saw when they went where they went. Everything bothered him, and his mother watched him and seemed to know something about him that she wouldn't say.

He mimicked people to make her laugh, and then to make the others laugh. The laundry women with their West Indian accents—"Dem two head cabbage," he would say to the men at the stable. "Dem ten pound potato in a five-pound sack," and they would laugh and let him get up on the horses. Spanish Pete, who got things ready for market, had a music Joseph could copy in his voice, nonsense syllables that Master found especially hilarious—"*Cuesta la bombolino de los frijoles!*" he would exclaim to howls of laughter. Cassius might say something to one of the other men, and Joseph would repeat it back in Cassius's voice. "I come up behind her when she washin' Massa's dirty drawers and tell her how I likes it," and the other men would laugh and laugh, and Cassius would, too, unless Joseph did it a couple or three times and then Cassius would say, "What are you? A God damn mockingbird?"

He rarely saw the fields, or the slaves who worked the fields. A man named Mister Colson rode a horse and had a gun and came through once a day to talk to Master James. One time had one of the field slaves with him, had his shirt torn open on the side soaked with blood. Master hollering at him—"Don't bring this here! What's wrong with you?" And

Colson yelling back and then Colson left the farm, replaced by Nettles.

Joseph worked in the wood shop. Cassius said Joseph had an easy life, had nothing to complain about. Master didn't even come to the cabin anymore. When Joseph would walk down by the river and watch the boats, though, it weighed on his mind. Where did they go? Who was on them? The boats no longer a kind of decoration but part of a mechanism connected to something invisible that he was beginning to realize did not belong to Master James.

Enoch returned the next spring. He wore a red silk scarf around his neck and had on real trousers. More important, he had a musical instrument with him. Joseph had never bothered about music one way or the other, although he had an ear for spoken language. This was something different, though.

Enoch said it was a banjar. A large round hoop with a skin over it, the skin held in place by a metal ring with shiny brass bolts. The neck was a rich cherry red and it tapered up to the head, which scrolled and curled around itself. The polished wood shone. As soon as Enoch played a note, Joseph was free. The sound was freedom. Enoch played two or three simple, rhythmic songs. Where you thought there would be a note, there would be no note. Then when you thought a silence, a note tapped you on the back of the head; when you turned around, it was gone.

One day, after weeks of begging, Enoch let Joseph hold the banjar. He was instantly flooded with a sense of presence and power. Joseph strummed the strings down.

"Do one at a time," Enoch said. "This way." Showed him how to press down with his fingernail and snap the string, like flicking away a fly from a cake. Press and flick. Joseph did it, and a note bloomed, dark as molasses, with something peppery in its center. Joseph listened to the note slowly fade. He did another. Like breathing. He was lost to the room and the world until Enoch said, "That's all you do today."

Joseph looked up, almost panicked. "Show me."

"You come back sometime late and I'll show you."

He quickly learned the few tunes Enoch had to teach him. He would sit and play for as long as Enoch would let him, sometimes snapping down with his fingernail as Enoch had taught him, and sometimes plucking with his thumb and up with his forefinger. The sound of the notes, each one flaring up as he plucked it and then dying down and fading away, to be replaced by another, and another.

He learned songs from Marcellus, one about Black Mattie that his mother told him not to sing, and from one of the laundry women, about the bullfrog dressed in soldier clothes. He found that by turning around some of the finger patterns in the little tunes he could make new songs.

Master James had him play for visitors. There were glittering parties where the best silver and crystal were set out (after being meticulously polished by the servants, including his mother). After dinner, Joseph would be called in under the chandeliers to play and sing. The ladies wore cloth gowns, and two of the men had stains on their waistcoats. "What a prize he is!" one of the ladies said. Everyone looked at Joseph while he performed, and he liked it. The others were unseen, removing the plates, setting out dessert, but he was seen.

His mother's hair was going gray, and her legs were slightly bowed, and she was not yet thirty. She kept a rag doll on her sagging bed; she had had it since she was a girl. Master had given it to her, before she was old enough for him to use and then discard. Now she slept with the doll. Her treasures were a Bible that Mistress had given her before the trouble started, and out of which she had learned to read, and a few trinkets, tiny presents from Master—a little tea cup—cracked and then glued together—a hand mirror with a pearly frame. A small ceramic dog. One day, Joseph, fifteen years old, asked her where they came from and she told him they were gifts from Master, with a kind of pride. By that time Joseph had figured out the business Master had had with her. Astonished, furious, he asked how she could keep the trinkets after what he had done. Because they are pretty, she said. They are mine. That damn drunk, he said. She looked as if she were going to slap him, then she turned, shaking her head, put the things in order on the small table by her bed.

He suffered attacks of melancholy, of suffocating sadness. To combat the feeling, he played the banjo for himself. It consoled him. Why it did, he could not say. Alone, he had a brother in the banjo. For others, he played musical jokes, tricks, sleight of hand. The visitors mistook it for simple happiness.

Aurora liked to watch him play and that did not hurt, either. Tired of thinking about her by himself in the rushes, one day he got her an hour before dinner and asked her to take a walk with him.

"Where you want to go?" she said, making it clear with her eyes that she knew.

Looking once over her shoulder they walked slowly past the number two barn and the smokehouse and then started running when they knew they were out of sight.

It became a constant torment to him. For three weeks they met, becoming increasingly reckless in their meetings. Until one day she failed to show up for a rendezvous and Joseph went looking for her. He couldn't find her at the dairy, he couldn't find her at the Upper Quarters. He went to barn number two and couldn't find her there either.

He saw her the next day, walking quickly from the Mansion House toward the Upper Quarters, and he ran to catch up with her. She wouldn't talk to him or even look at him, and when he grabbed her arm she shook him away almost violently and quickened her step away from him, leaving him standing there like a scarecrow. The talk got around that she was now living in the Mansion House, Master's newest "keep Miss."

When Marcellus told him, in a tone half-amused, as if to say Welcome to the world as it is, Joseph looked at the face, with its lines, its mustache, and felt something fall off a table in his mind, as if a wind had pushed it, and the next thing he realized, Cassius was pulling him off of Marcellus and holding him as Joseph struggled to hit him, or anyone, anything. Marcellus, who had fallen backward, took the opportunity to stand back up and slap Joseph hard, open-hand, across the face. "Your own Daddy doing your girl." Joseph lunged at him again, and Cassius had to drag Joseph out of the stable and pin him on the ground until he stopped fighting and started weeping.

Later that afternoon, he returned to the cabin he shared with his mother, with his shirt ripped and his clothes disarranged.

His mother asked him what was wrong with him, and she got it out of him without much trouble.

"I am going to kill him," he said.

She got a frightened look on her face and said, "You do that, you kill me."

Gradually, the edge of anger wore down enough for Joseph to think clearly, and that was when he began to think about escape. Enoch told him the names of two other slaves on the farm, hire-outs from Belle View, who were connected with people and who could get word to them and help Joseph escape. It took nearly two long months in the autumn. One day, a man he did not recognize approached the cabin. The man pulled something from under his shirt and set it down inside the cabin door and left without a word. Joseph never saw him again. It was a packet containing some papers and an address in Wilmington, Delaware. Across the top of the page with the address were written the words "MEMORISE AND BURN."

The night Joseph left The Tides was clear and cold. He had packed two suits of clothes, some linen, a small loaf of bread, some cured salt pork, and three pairs of socks—a luxury. His banjo he carried in a cinch bag made from a grain sack. He carried two other items as well. Out of Master's lodge room that evening he had taken a pair of new leather boots that he planned to wear; his other shoes were in his carry sack, along with the copy of *David Copperfield* that he had stolen from Master's library. In his jacket he had a sharp knife in a goatskin sheath for protection, and in his breeches pocket a small folding pocketknife.

Joseph was to light out for the river when the moon cleared the eastern tree line and then head north, walking at a steady pace until the moon was halfway across the sky, when he would come to a boathouse. He would need money, about fifteen dollars, a not inconsiderable sum. The boatman would then tell him what his next steps would be.

At the last moment he had been affected with pangs of loss and misgivings. The cabin he shared with his mother was comfortable and familiar. Above all, his mother's arms and reassuring voice. As he lay warm in his bed for the last time, waiting, part of him rebelled and wanted only to stay there, warm, and not go out under the cold night sky on a trip with no end. Finally his mother shook him by the shoulder, and Joseph said, quietly, "I'm awake." He sat up, already fully dressed, and put on the boots.

"Those belong to him," she said.

"No more," Joseph said, tying them.

She sat, watching her son prepare to leave. He tried to show no weakness that would make her doubt his readiness, and she made the same effort.

"You have the money I put up?"

"Yes," he said. "Inside here."

When he was ready he hefted up his sack, which had a strap she had sewn on, for slinging over his shoulder. It was heavier than he would have liked, but it contained necessities. Before he picked up his banjo, he and his mother looked at one another by the dim light of the one candle.

"You go," she said.

He had planned to be strong, afraid of breaking down and losing his resolve. But at the last moment he put down

the bag and came to his mother, who closed her eyes as if
she had wanted to avoid a final goodbye. He embraced her;
her body was rigid with the attempt to resist the grief this
moment brought. After a moment, one arm went up behind
his back and she held him to her, strong at first, then more
strongly. Then she said only, "Don't let them catch you. Ever.
Go now."

He picked up his bag again, and the sack with the banjo,
and he made his way to the back door of the cabin, and before
he could turn around to look at her again she blew out the
candle and the room went dark.

He walked miles of shore, making his way along the forested
banks. There were two long stretches of open land where he
was able to make good time, but where he was also exposed
in the moonlight. He was too intent to be frightened; all his
senses were alert, focused on the single goal of reaching the
boathouse. He wore the hunting boots and carried his other
shoes in his bag because they were lighter. When the moon
was high up overhead, he came to a small creek, and, across
it, saw the low house with three rowboats tied up alongside.

They had not told him what to do when he reached the
house, and there was no light in the window. He sat among
the trees and watched and listened; the sound of the trickling
creek was time itself running through the night, and finally
he decided to cross at a narrow place and knock on the cabin
door. He knocked very softly and watched for a light to go on.
At length a door opened into a dark interior and a voice said
only, "Walk to the second boat and wait."

The rowboat wobbled as he stepped in, and he kept his weight low, sat down. After a few minutes the boatman appeared, got in, requested Joseph's money, and pushed off. After the initial transaction they didn't speak, and as the overhanging trees gave way to the starry sky and they moved away across the water under the immense vault and he saw the land retreating behind them, falling away, he felt the size of what he was doing, suddenly exposed and vulnerable, for the first time.

On the far shore they tied up and the man told him where to walk, following the banks of the Choptank, told him about a series of landmarks, and then how to find his way to Delaware. As the boatman made ready to leave, Joseph nearly asked to be carried back across; he allowed himself to imagine going back overland and making it home to the farm before daylight. And as he imagined it, he knew he would not do it, and that he would never go back.

Four more nights walking until the first hints of coming light in the sky, the first birds darting across a treetop to a barn, and days sleeping in cold barns and in the woods—he had never been so cold—first along the Choptank and through Tidewater Maryland, making his way by the stars, then Delaware, and a bed for a night in Wilmington with people who gave him identification papers and a new name— Henry Sims—and directions to an address in Philadelphia. A morning steamer carried him up the Delaware River, finally docking at the foot of Arch Street in the late afternoon. From the top of a hill the lowering sun blazed into his eyes amid a tangle of noise, shouted orders, cart wheels on cobblestones. He stepped off the packet boat to take his first steps on solid ground as a free man.

Experience was instantly more dense. Walking up the hill from the river—the shops, the signs for stoves, shoes, rope, eyeglasses . . . Everything was someone's idea, everything was multiplied. The sky took less of the world, replaced by buildings. There were alleys and walls and places to hide, to appear and disappear. The last of the most recent snow still blurred the streets and superimposed webs of pointless lines, maps of nonexistent terrain, a second skin. In Virginia when snow covered the ground it revealed clear footprints, showed where one had walked. Here your footsteps would be constantly erased, and that was fine with him. There were overlapping rhythms, constantly changing patterns. That much was instantly clear.

He climbed the hill, found Fifth Street, and turned right on a shadowy sidewalk, following the directions he had committed to memory. Numbers, which he knew, as he knew how to read words, from his mother. The houses needed the numbers. Not The Tides' smokehouse, dairy, washhouse, wood shop, blacksmith. Instead, the numbers that ordered everything, implied a progress.

A door the color of dried blood opened onto a short woman with blue-black skin, who gave him an approving once-over.

"Mister Still gone for the day." She spoke in a West Indian accent that he recognized; three of the house women at The Tides were from there. They had a little society of their own, laughing and chattering like magpies over the laundry, nonstop. "He know you was coming?" Someone said something from a room beyond and she laughed.

An oil painting, oil lamps, narrow stairway going up on the left, carpeted. A mirror.

"Wait here," the woman said. "Where you came from?"

"Virginia."

"I got cousin family there. What you got in that bag?"

"A banjo," Henry said.

"Ooooh. Play me a song. Them Quaker don't like music, no."

A large, very black man appeared in the doorway from the back room, saying, "Please get finished so we can go home."

Looking at Henry, the woman said, "You going to have lots of company. Listen to what Sam say—him boss man 'til Mister Still come. You play me a song sometime?"

When she disappeared, the man named Sam addressed Henry, saying, "You were on the packet boat, from Wilmington?"

"Yes," Henry said.

"Mister Still will receive you tomorrow." He looked Henry up and down and said he needed warmer clothes.

"Either that or warmer weather," Henry said.

"I will get a coat for you," Sam said, unsmiling. He turned his head to holler something into the back room, where the voices were chattering, and Henry noticed a long, raised scar on the back of his neck. "Wait here."

Sam returned and led Henry to a house three blocks away, and down a couple of cement stairs to a door that opened into a basement passageway lined with exposed rocks. Sam stepped inside a doorway to the left and got a lamp lit; there was a simple bed with a basin and a towel and a water jug, full. Some paintings leaning against the wall with their backs to the room, two steamer trunks, pipes overhead. There was a damp smell, but it was warm.

"They had eighteen to come through just in the last four days," Sam said. "You'll be all right here for a night. You remember the way back to the office."

"Two streets down, one to the right."

"Number three-six-four," Sam said. "The bells will tell you what time it is."

When Sam had left, Henry sat on the bed. He listened for footfalls, conversation, any hints from the floor above his head, but he heard nothing. On the bedside table, a small box with a brass latch and a carving of a cross on top. He picked it up, set it back down. A brass candle holder shaped like a flower, with a taper burned to within two inches. Picked it up, set it back down, looked around. Right now, he thought, Mama is in the house, mending clothes. Enoch is in the shed, sorting rope or wiping down tools. He pulled off the boots, which had raised several blisters, but he kept every other piece of clothing on, hat included.

Quietly, he pulled the banjo out of its sack, set it on his lap, and softly sounded the strings, one at a time, adjusted the tuning, sounded them again. He played no pattern; a pattern would come later. He sounded each string softly and let it fade in turn.

The next morning he awoke, still in his clothes. A thin, horizontal wedge of sunlight struggled into the room through a shallow window at street level, dirty enough to obscure a view of the outside world. Carts passing on the street, people walking, voices. His bag was in the corner, where he had put it, and the banjo.

A piece of paper had been slid under his door; on it, an arrow, pointing toward the door and the hallway through which he had entered.

He pulled the bed covers up, straightened them. A mount-ing feeling of excitement. He was in Philadelphia. Not on the farm, not hiding in a barn. Tentatively, he raised the iron latch and opened the thin wooden door to find a tray on the hallway floor. On it, a plate with a towel covering two corn muffins, and next to it a glass of milk.

It was time to head to Mr. Still's office, and the people who would help him. He picked up his duffel and the bag con-taining his banjo and, with a look around, quit the room and walked up the stairs and out into the morning.

Henry was reading the spines on a wall of bookshelves in a large room that also contained a broad desk and a table cov-ered with neat stacks of papers, three heavy wooden chairs deployed around it. The door opened and Henry turned, holding a volume in his hand, to see a tall, clean-shaven, el-egantly dressed man who regarded him with a kind smile. Henry had assumed that such an important man would be white, and it took him some moments to realize that his bene-factor was, in fact, a Negro.

"Have you found something of interest?" Closed the door behind him. Noting the familiar cover, William Still said, "Dickens was here, some years ago."

Astonished, Henry said, "In this room?"

"In Philadelphia," the forgiving reply. "Who taught you to read?"

"My mother." The books smuggled one by one out of Mas-ter's library, then replaced. Except for one. Sounding out the words by the wavering candlelight.

"Please . . ." The man gestured to a chair and walked around his desk to seat himself. Henry took the proffered seat, still holding on to the book, a copy of *Barnaby Rudge*.

The great man asked Henry a number of questions about where he had come from, if he had been misused, taking notes on his story as Henry spoke. Mr. Still asked Henry about the banjo, then he laid out the various means of getting to Canada.

Henry had heard about Canada—some of the slaves at The Tides had called it "Canaan," and the family in Wilmington had assumed that he was bound for Canada. But Henry did not want to go there, and he said this. Canada he pictured as a cold place, with no trees, where people tended a few tomato plants and read the Bible and wrote letters of gratitude. "I want to stay in Philadelphia," he said.

William Still drew a measured breath and said, "You must realize that you could be captured at any moment and brought back to Virginia."

"I won't go back," Henry said.

"The only way to make certain of that is to continue on to Canada." Still paused. "You're free to do what you want—of course—but this is how things stand. You or any other Negro—whether under title to a slave owner or not—is in danger of being captured and taken south as long as he is in this country. Moreover, it is a crime for citizens not to aid in that capture if asked. This is now the law of the land. This city has many sympathizers with our cause, but you are not safe if someone comes to reclaim you."

"You haven't been captured," Henry said.

After a moment's surprise, Still replied, "I am known, and I would be too easily recognized."

Recognized, Henry thought. "What do they do in Canada?"

"They farm, or they run businesses of their own. They raise families. They do what any other human being is allowed to do, or should be allowed to do by natural right, here in the United States. They lead their lives. Perhaps you imagine being there alone, but there are already thriving communities of our people, who live free of the threat of the lash. Hundreds of them. I imagine your master will come looking for you."

"He is not my master."

"Yes," Still said, holding up his hand. "I misspoke."

William Still said that if Henry would not go to Canada, he could perhaps be of use in Philadelphia, speaking at meetings. He said he would arrange for Henry to stay with a white family named Passmore, temporarily, and he directed Sam to bring him there. "Hilda will provide you with some fresh clothes."

Henry was still holding on to the book and he held it out to Mr. Still.

"Would you like to borrow it?"

"I'll return it," Henry said.

"I know you will."

In the evenings the Passmores sat by lamplight, quiet, the Bible reading. Their son, seven years old. Robert Allen Passmore. Always addressed as Robert Allen. On the second night, Henry caught his eye. "Here," Henry said, presenting the two open, upward-facing palms of his hands, the right hand displaying a copper disc. "Here is a penny. I'll let you keep it if you can tell me which hand has it after I've closed my fists."

An eager nod from the boy.

"Watch closely, now." The boy's attention focused on his hands.

"Now!" and with a rapid snap of the wrists the hands flipped, clenched, palms downward now, awaiting the verdict. The boy tapped the right hand, where he had last seen the coin, the obvious choice. Henry righted his hands upward and opened them to reveal—but how?—the penny on the left palm. The boy in transports of wonder and delight. Henry noticed the glance that went between the boy's parents; it was not approving.

During the day, he walked. No one accosted him; no one seemed even to notice him. Everything about the city made him hungry. He would walk all the way into town, fascinated, then come back to the Passmores', invigorated and tired. Theaters, factories, stores for tools, eyeglasses, wigs, stoves, steam engines, trunks, satchels, carpetbags; liquors, coal, candles, bells, chocolates, feathers, clocks, boots, books, coffee, rope . . . Standing in front of the bakery on Third and Market, sugar on his chin, sun on his face, he savored the pure and undefiled moment.

Springtime came early that year. Mr. Passmore brought him to a chair maker on Second Street, a friend of the abolitionist cause, who let Henry work for several weeks, cleaning up and doing some finishing work. With the money he made there he moved out of the Passmores' house—they had offered to keep him on as a servant, but he declined. Sam had told him about Bottle Alley, which was run by a friend of Sam's named Zena.

When he arrived in Bottle Alley, Henry felt more comfortable. All the occupants were Negroes, for one thing. There was an open courtyard, hidden from street view, with a dirt floor and a pump for water. There were chickens walking around and always at least a couple of occupants sitting on a bench, making conversation. Jerome was a regular fixture—a dark-skinned man with perpetually red eyes who smelled of whiskey. When Henry said hello to him the first time and asked him how he was, he replied, "Still a nigger," which was how he replied every time he was asked. Zena did laundry and cooking out there as well, a large-boned, very black woman with a vicious-looking scar down the left cheekbone that continued down her neck to her collarbone. She wore a wooden whistle on a leather cord around her neck. Zena was matter-of-fact about everything, stood for no nonsense from anyone, but she was honest, and Henry liked her. He asked her if it was all right if he played his banjo in the evenings, and she had looked at him as if he were crazy.

"Go on play your banjo," she said, frowning as if he were trying to put something over on her. "I don't give a God damn, and if anybody doesn't like it tell them to see me." She surprised Henry, a few days later, as he was passing through the courtyard on his way somewhere, by asking with characteristic abruptness, "What song was that you was just playing?"

"The last one?" Henry had said. "That was 'Black Betty.' You like that one?"

"'Black Betty,'" she said, as if memorizing instructions. Then, "Why else I ask you if I didn't like it?"

People kept to themselves in Bottle Alley. No one asked where you came from or why you were there or where you were going, and that suited Henry fine. His room had no lock, nor even a knob or latch; only a crude hook-and-eye to keep the door shut while he was out. No one there had much of anything, and theft was not a problem. With the dirt floor and the scrawny tree, the chickens Zena kept, it all reminded him of The Tides, but in a pleasant way, as if Master James weren't a part of it. A little patch of the country in the middle of the city. The easy comfort of other black folks.

Outside, on the streets, he was invisible. No one saw you unless you gave them a reason to see you. You could watch people going about their business, study their faces as if you were a ghost. That was something you could use to your advantage. Even as he realized this, he was beginning to need something more. The one good thing about The Tides was the opportunity to perform, to be seen and admired. He wanted that now, as he became used to Philadelphia. He wanted to see where it could lead. Slowly at first, testing, he began spying out likely places to perform. Playing for the parties at The Tides had taught him how to make people laugh, make them dance, make them wistful. Twice he had gone as a valet with Stephens to Richmond and watched very closely at the musicales they had attended. And he had seen traveling shows, and there had been a hand who worked at The Tides for a few months, and of course, the few things Enoch had taught him. He learned quickly, and he remembered what he had learned.

He found a spot near the foot of Chesnut Street by the Black Horse Tavern and, later, one down by Spruce Street, and another at the top of Callowhill. Each one offered nearby alleys and other possible escape routes should trouble appear.

Playing on the street was an education in what people wanted, what they expected, and the range of responses when you subverted those expectations. What kept their attention and what did not, and what kind of attention you wanted. There was power that came, like magic, when you performed. Time expanded, changed shape, slowed down so that once he cast the spell he could move, unseen, while his listeners sat, bound by the illusion he spun, as if they were listening to someone else. You had to divide yourself. First there was one of you and many of them; then there was one of them, and many of you. At the same time, you kept something private that nobody could see or touch. It was a way to live. He knew that this power could end up being a vulnerability, as if he were daring the world to call him by his right name.

And now, this James Douglass. He didn't ask Henry too many questions, and that was a good thing. At certain moments, Henry found himself relaxing with him, enjoying a joke or sharing some observation; then he'd pull himself back, as if he had fallen asleep while riding a horse. You could never take off the mask.

And there was the girl. One day he thought he saw her, walking on the street, and he followed until she stepped into a doorway between two shops on Walnut Street. He could not follow her inside, of course, but in his mind he did. All afternoon he followed her in his mind. Was that where she was "kept"? Where she let the fiddler have his way? He wanted her to see him, think about him, watch him. He was tired of being invisible. In a short time, he would perform onstage, in a real theater. It was nobody's idea of what he was, or what he would do. You were free as long as you chose your own mask. The more masks, the better. He would not be one more of everybody, subject to the same vanishing. He would not vanish.

7

Rose and I both arrived early on the night of the performance to make sure that all was in order. There was a service entrance around back of the theater, and I told Henry to come in that way around five thirty, so there would be no chance of his being seen and stopped. Rose had outdone herself with Henry's costume. It was worthy of Sweeney. She got the idea perfectly. She had whipped up a confection of long, silver-and-green-striped satin breeches, a white shirt with enormous green dots, a red bow tie, and an orange plaid jacket that was intentionally too large, but with the sleeves shortened so as not to interfere with his banjo playing. I had described Sweeney's top hat, and she had replicated that as well.

I paced restlessly, running through the scenarios over and over. Rose and I had gotten everything necessary laid out in her workroom. I imported a jar of blacking from the troupe's sanctum, along with a wig and some other items; we would make Henry up in Rose's room, before the members of the troupe arrived, so I could present him as a fait accompli.

As five thirty drew near, I walked back and forth, through the area where we stored some unused sets and drops, double-checking to make certain that the rear entrance was open. Just after the half-hour struck, Henry rounded the edge of a building into the alley that led to the rear entrance. He carried his banjo in its sack, and he wore a cloth jacket with the collar turned up and a wool cap pulled low on his forehead, a somewhat dramatic touch. Henry, like Rose, had a faculty for the theatrical in every-day life. I ushered him in and closed the door.

"Are you ready?" I said, as we made our way through the lost harbor of stage sets back toward Rose's room.

"Yes," he said. He was otherwise quiet as we walked, and it seemed to me that he was holding something very close inside. I couldn't imagine what was going through his mind. I was silently running through a list of other details myself, hoping that the reporter from the *Bee* would be there; I had tipped him off that we had a new attraction that I thought he might enjoy.

In Rose's room we began our preparations. Henry and Rose seemed rather shy around each other, and I tried to warm the atmosphere with some chatter, showing Henry the fine points of the costume, the wig, all of it. He undressed behind a screen in the corner to don his stage trousers and shirt. Then he stepped out, and Rose and I helped him with the rest of it, tucking and pinning. We left the shirt unfas-tened at the top, and Rose placed a towel around his neck, like a collar, and we got him seated at a small table in front of a looking glass to get him blacked up.

I showed him the technique—three fingers, held together and flat, so as to apply the cork evenly, in succes-
sive, incremental arcs following the curves of the jawline
and cheekbones—and he set to work applying it under our
gaze. I saw him look at himself before applying the first
swipe, as if he were looking at a friend who was depart-
ing for a long journey. His copper-colored skin, the long
eyelashes, the green eyes. He brushed his fingers across
the surface of the coal-dark mixture and, watching himself
eye-to-eye, spread a first swath of black across his forehead, then a next one, and I watched him slowly transform
himself. When he had finished, with a couple of touch-ups
suggested by Rose, he sat staring at himself in the glass for
several moments.

I retrieved the wig from a stand on another table, slipped
the netting of tight black curls over Henry's own hair, adjusted it slightly. We all three regarded his image in the glass.

"Now you're one of us!" I said.

He looked at me in the mirror with a cryptic smile, barely
more than a glint in his eyes.

I left Henry and Rose and headed back to the dressing room,
where Mulligan and Burke were getting themselves ready.
Shortly after I entered, Eagan and Powell found their way in,
and we all got down to the business of remaking ourselves.

"Tonight is the night for the Banjo Phantom, isn't it?"
Burke asked.

I said that it was.

"Where is he?" Powell asked.

"We had to get him fitted down at Rose's," I said, noting a quick alertness from Eagan. "He is pathetically shy, I think because of the language barrier as much as anything. I'll retrieve him and bring him in so everyone may get acquainted before curtain."

"It would not have been a bad idea to rehearse beforehand," Eagan said, not looking at me.

"It was not in the cards this time, Michael," I said. "At any rate, all we have is some patter, and then he will step out front, do his tune, and that will be that. Not much rehearsal needed. We've been through this, haven't we?"

Mulligan was being quiet and even a bit sulky, I thought.

When I was blacked up and dressed I walked back to Rose's room, where Rose was laughing at something. Henry sat upon the edge of the divan, with one leg jiggling up and down.

"Well," I said. "Time."

We were within view of the dressing room now, and we held up walking.

"I told them you were very shy about meeting them," I said, running through our plan one last time. "You just smile and nod. I'll act as if I'm translating, and we'll converse in our false Spanish, and we'll see what transpires."

"You're sure none of them understands Spanish?" Henry said.

"Not this crew."

"Tell me again about the others."

"All right," I said. "Mulligan I told you about; he's sure to be a bit jealous of you, so be as solicitous as your language limitations will allow."

Henry nodded.

"Then there's Powell, on tambourine—I'll introduce them, no need to remember it all. Eagan and Burke . . . All right, now"—the dressing room door was ajar, across a section of backstage—"Spanish it is."

I walked into the open door, and Henry waited outside.

"Gentlemen," I announced, "please meet Juan García. Juan?" I looked toward the door. "He's very shy. Juan?"

Into the room Henry stepped, long-legged, tentative, like a heron wading into an unfamiliar pond, carrying his banjo, eyes wide, a scared grin on his face, his lurid satin costume a hallucination in a room full of comic tuxedos. The men, all of whom had applied the cork to their own faces, stared at him from behind the black masks.

"*Buenos tardes, señores*," Henry said, in creditable enough Spanish.

They stared at him through a long moment of strained silence.

"What is this, Douglass? A joke?" This was Eagan.

"Certainly not," I replied.

Predictably, Powell was the first to take things on face-value. He leaned back in his chair and offered his hand to Henry. "Pleased to meet you, brother. Dan Powell."

Henry looked into the man's eyes. "*Mucho gusto*," he said, bowing. "*Juan García.*"

Burke and Eagan then greeted Henry, Burke with some amusement, Eagan rather coldly.

The last of them was Mulligan, who had remained seated. Noting his resistance, I stepped in, saying, "And the man who never learned manners, seated there, is John Mulligan."

Henry popped his eyes wide, looked back and forth between Mulligan and myself. *"Mulligan? Eso?"* Mulligan, squinting, watched Henry and me, in succession.

I nodded.

Turning to Mulligan, Henry launched into a torrent of self-abasing pidgin. *"Señor . . . que tenga las banderilleras de todos los arboles y cuatros bolantes infinitas, a las sombras . . . a las montañas . . . el nombre de Mulligan es lo bandito sobresaliente de la playa de banjo, los palabras de los cojones prodigiosas . . ."* on and on, that left Mulligan frowning and looking to me for aid.

"I couldn't catch all of it," I said. "But I think he said that you are his hero, the greatest banjo player who ever lived, and that your fame has spread even to his country."

Mulligan seemed to soften slightly, offered his hand from his sitting position, and said, "Obliged. Welcome to America."

There ensued a few moments of silence, and then the fellows began to turn back to the task of preparing themselves for the night's show, and I joined them.

"Douglass, where do you learn to speak Spanish?"

"He's not Mexican. Not with the green eyes. Who is he, really, Douglass?"

Mulligan was tuning his banjo, an elaborately carved instrument with a scroll on the head and inlaid wood up and down the fingerboard. I watched Henry regard the banjo with something like awe. The banjo tuned, Mulligan exercised himself with a number of quick and very dexterous runs up and down the fingerboard, ending with several variations on "Essence of Old Virginny." Henry looked across the room at me, and I shot him a look that said, He may be an ass sometimes, but he can play the banjo. Henry nodded and smiled.

"*Qué escabeche!*" he said.

"You like that, eh?" Mulligan said. "Let's see yours."

Remembering to feign incomprehension, Henry smiled and nodded.

Mulligan said, "Tell him I want to see his banjo."

I made gestures to this effect, and Henry handed his banjo to Mulligan, who took it, turned it to look inside the rim, examined the head, the joining of the neck to the rim, the peghead. Satisfied, he flipped the instrument around into position and threw off a few runs quickly, then a very fast version of some little rhythmic bagatelle. He nodded once, brought it to a stop, and handed it back to Henry, whose face expressed ecstasy.

"Not bad," Mulligan said, "Now you play something."

"*Tocar,*" I offered, from across the room.

Feigning consternation, and after a few protests, Henry played a restrained version of the "Grapevine Twist." I watched Mulligan's expression—one of pleasure, since the level of skill on display was just below his, although obviously of high competence. Henry was nothing if not competitive, however; he came to the final chorus and between two of the melody lines slipped in a very tricky phrase that involved raking down across the strings with the nail of his index finger and somehow inserting two perfectly timed thumb plucks on the high string as he did it. A quick frown crossed Mulligan's face and I could almost hear Henry think, "My compliments." He was not able to finish before Mulligan interrupted.

"Here," Mulligan said, "how did you do that?"

Henry looked at him helplessly, looked over at me, back at Mulligan. "*Qué?*" he said, pathos itself.

I told Henry in pidgin what Mulligan said, and Henry responded in an elaborate sentence that ended in a look of supplication.

"I believe he said that he doesn't know how he did it," I said. "He plays purely by instinct."

"Instinct," Mulligan said, turning back to the dressing table. "Huh."

Henry remained backstage during our first half. The show went well; the theater was only about two-thirds full, but the crowd was noisily appreciative, raucous even, and I hoped Henry wouldn't be thrown by the occasional shout or unceremonious address from the balcony. We had a stock of ripostes ready to use in response to any wit in the audience, and we could certainly pick up the slack if Henry were momentarily unsettled.

The half ended with "Across the Sea," and we were borne offstage on a tide of whistles and hollers and applause. We made straight for the dressing room, where we had fifteen minutes to refresh ourselves, confer, touch up our corking, and make any costume changes that might be necessary. The audience, during that time, was invited to buy beer and spirits in the lobby, and our second half was always more boisterous than the first on the other side of the proscenium.

Henry was there in the dressing room, and I ran through the setup for the second half, reminding everyone of the routine, with Henry sitting stage right, in back until I cued Powell to ask me who he was. Henry pretended not to understand, and I told everyone that I had walked him through and explained it to him already, with difficulty.

When it was time, we all made our way to the stage, where the curtain was down. From the other side we could hear the excited rumble and stirring of the audience; I might almost have been as tense as Henry must have felt. I got him situated—chair stage right, rear, but angled so that I could watch him and either send or receive a signal if needed.

We got ourselves arranged in the front line, which occupied a shallow concavity almost against the curtain, and we sat, adjusting our suits and composing ourselves. Eagan, thumbing his strings, made slight tuning adjustments, Mulligan the same. I glanced back at Henry, wondering what was going through his mind, encountering this roar behind the curtain, as if on the other side were a vast stockyard of restless animals. The sound was oceanic, textured yet indistinct; periodically a voice would rise out of the general boil and become a dominant theme for a few moments, to be joined by another and then be swallowed up in a general babble again. This, I thought, must indeed have been what the Greek army felt like, massed inside the Trojan horse, waiting for the gangplank to drop. I saw Henry run his thumb very lightly over his strings to check the tuning one more time.

The noise from out front abated slightly, suddenly, then reached a new crescendo of applause, hollers, and catcalls, which slowly eased down as a voice arose from the other side of the curtain—Gilman, our house manager and master of ceremonies, announcing the second half. We all straightened up, faced the curtain directly in front of us, and got our instruments into position.

"Ladies and gentlemen," Gilman began. "It is my great pleasure once again . . ."

A voice from the audience hollered, "I'm no gentleman!" and the theater was again awash in hollers and whoops.

"Ladies and gentlemen," Gilman rode in again, over the din, "*and the talking jackass in row twenty-five!*" and was drowned out now by an even louder wave of approval, hollers, laughter, and shrieks. "Welcome once again to Barton's Theatre, where only the finest in entertainment may be found. To-*NIGHT* it is our pleasure—nay, our great privilege—to present once again the sensation of the age, the toast of three continents, the preeminent delineators of Ethiopian melodies, here, for their second act—the *Virginia Harmonists!*"

A tidal wave rolled in over the final syllables, submerging the entire world under applause, screams, and hollers, a wall of sound, almost physical in its force. I stomped four times with my whole leg to set the rhythm visually for the others, since it was impossible to hear, and we launched into "Jenny Get Your Hoe Cake Done" as the curtain rose slowly in front of us to reveal a mob, cheering, cupping their hands around their mouths, some standing on the seats, clapping their hands over their heads, as far back into the cavernous hall as one could see.

I glanced quickly at Henry, who sat, slack-jawed, in his chair staring vacantly out at the audience, as we had planned it. Behind that mask, what was he seeing? What was he thinking? As I sang and played the bones, I saw and heard it through his eyes and ears—the five of us in the front line—angles, elbows, knees, bouncing—*whack* on the tambourine; bones clicking and arms crisscrossing on and off the beat; the banjo and the fiddle neck and neck with one another as the line sang the familiar song. Although the noise from the audience drowned us out at first, I fancied that one could have all but heard the music from the interplay of our gestures and motions alone. The audience gazed up at the five men in blackface in our front line with the kind of adoration and even ecstasy that must have greeted Napoleon riding with a conquering army.

The opener finished, we rode directly in on top of the applause with "River Man," the five of us singing in our famous harmony:

If I could sing like a river man
I'd take mah Lucy by de hand
Up and down de riverside
Me de husband, she de bride . . .

Eagan played the "Virginia Reel," which we could not get away without performing, Mulligan essayed "Essence of Old Virginny," to which he added a perceptible increment of bravado—spurred, I am sure, by Henry's, or Demosthenes', presence. I had moved "Fire Down Below" to the first half, and instead we placed Burke, as Brother Rastus, at this point in the second half, to deliver one of his signature monologues in rhyme, half-spoken, half-sung, full of pathos. He quieted the applause that followed on Mulligan by rising and shouting, "*Cease!*"

The audience immediately began to settle down, and when Burke hollered "*Cease!*" once more, they were paying attention.

"*I has a mournful story to tell you now,*" Brother Rastus began.

"*And de way you tells it is eben mo' mournful,*" Brother Scamp—Eagan—shouted. Laughter, hoots of derision from the audience.

Short-lived, though, because Burke was a favorite, and the crowd knew what to expect.

"*Peace be unto you, Brother Scamp. Hold your criticalism until I'se finished wit' my tale of woe.*"

A silence descended now as Burke began.

In Old Virginny, way down South,
I left Old Master there,
And dear old kindly Missus
In her favorite rocking chair.

They were so kind and good to me
But home I would not stay.
I left the old Plantation;
I up and ran away.

I went up North to Boston
And there I made my home
'Mongst barren trees and frozen lakes
And thought no more to roam.

But many nights I dreamt about
The old plantation days
When Master let me serve the guests
On sparkling silver trays.

I longed to see my brothers
And taste a mincemeat pie
And frolic at the quarters
With the girls who caught my eye.

And then one day a letter came
And then my spirits fell.
It read, "Oh Rastus, hurry home;
Old Master is not well."

I thought of dear old happy days,
Of all the times we had;
I packed my trunk and headed South;
I thought I would go mad.

It was a soft and sunny day
When I hobbled through the gate.
Dear old Mistress greeted me,
"Praise God, you're not too late."

Up the stairs we fairly flew
To Master's sad bedside.
And when I met him lying there,
Old Mistress, how she cried.

But Master, hearing Rastus' voice
His eyes he opened wide.
"Oh Lord, my prayers are answered!"
And drew me to his side.

"I thought that I should never see
Another happy day,"
He said through shining, blessed tears,
And then he passed away.

And now I live and ne'er shall leave
And never shall I roam.
I'll serve my dear old Mistress
'Til God shall call me home.

There were no hoots or hollers now. All faces were turned to the stage as if toward the setting sun, full of wonder, nostalgia, regret, several of the men weeping openly.

The show went on. Henry sat still as a tombstone in his chair, staring out into the hall like a half-wit. I saw one or two audience members take tentative note of him. He was perspiring, and the rim of his crushed top hat showed a darkened line of dampness along the base of the crown. We next tore into "De Boatman Dance," always a crowd-pleaser. One man, near the front, kept a close watch on whatever the lead performer was doing, and he appeared to be acting out in his own mind what he saw on the stage; emotions of pathos and mirth alternated, as if his face were controlled by the actions of the line. When Eagan sang "Boatman," the fellow sang along on the chorus—

. . . Hi ho, the boatman row
Down the river, the Ohio . . .

—slamming his hands on the back of the seat in front of him, which caused that seat's occupant to give him a remonstrative glare until he stopped. The man sitting next to him watched with a perfectly blank face, eyes wide, as if transfixed by a vision. Men swung their arms in time to the music, stomped on the floorboards, one man in the aisle danced a jig. On every face was reflected some aspiration, as if we in the line were liberating something in them, giving shape and voice to some hope or memory, some longing or wonder; they were like children watching a puppet show. In some, a strange anger mixed with the high spirits. One woman— there were very few women in the house—stood on a seat and hollered, "*You big black nigger! You God damn nigger!*" until the man next to her pulled her down, to their neighbors' riotous laughter.

What Henry could have made of all of this was anyone's guess. If he thought anything at all, he gave no sign, as he sat there with a look of pure idiocy on his face. On we played, Eagan on the fiddle, myself on the bones, Mulligan on the banjo . . . ourselves and yet not ourselves anymore, either—or had we in fact become our true selves, Scamp, Neckbones, Bullfrog? Who could say? We played and sang and danced under the audience's gaze, like five moons reflecting the sun's light, our other half hidden in unfathomable darkness.

Powell finished singing—"*I likes my hoe cakes brown in de mornin'.*" During the applause, I happened to glance toward the wings stage right, where I saw Gilman and, next to him, Rose, wearing a big smile. It was rare for her to watch a performance. Now Mulligan moved his chair slightly forward and it was my turn to announce him to the audience.

"*Kind peoples,*" I said, "*now de great Bullfrog Johnson is gwine to preform de 'Cornshuckin' Jig'!*"

"*Thank you, Brudder Neckbones,*" Mulligan said, launching into the virtuoso piece. He really poured it on, making all kinds of flourishes on the banjo, much to the crowd's vocal appreciation. I was sure this was a kind of preemptive show of dominance aimed at Henry. Rose was laughing and hollering encouragement to Mulligan.

There was a sudden ripple of disturbance in the audience, attention toward stage right, and I turned and saw that Henry had collapsed in his chair. He was bent forward, his right leg thrown out in front of him. This alarmed me terribly, but a moment later I saw him snap back up exactly into his previous position, with the vacant expression on his face.

This attracted an audible reaction from the audience. Now I kept one eye on him as I clacked along with Mulligan, who had no idea what was causing the murmuring in the hall. Rose stood, in the wings, watching Henry with her hand over her mouth and an astonished expression on her face. Mulligan now returned to the song's first strain and executed one or two extravagantly ornamented variations. As he did so, Henry collapsed again, like a decommissioned marionette, throwing out his left leg now, and twisting to that side. Again he held still for a moment, then snapped back up into position.

Now a rise of laughter and quickened attention came off the audience, although the other men in our line, with their backs to Henry, had no idea of the source of the disturbance. Many eyes had shifted away from Mulligan to Henry. Sensing that something was afoot, Mulligan turned his head, but Henry was once again still as a statue, and he remained that way until the end of the song.

Another number, a fiddle feature for Eagan, was scheduled before Demosthenes Jones was to make his official debut, but under the circumstances I thought it best to initiate Henry's routine immediately. I would hear about it later from Eagan, I knew, but I saw little choice.

After Mulligan had finished and was taking his bow—to larger applause than usual—a voice from the back of the theater hollered, *"Who's the nigger with the St. Vitus Dance?"* A swell of approval ensued. I gave Powell the nod, and he stepped into the moment.

"Why, Brother Neckbones—who is dat nigger sittin' there watchin' while we does all de work?"

Widening my eyes and craning my neck around to regard the still-seated Henry, I replied, *"Why, Brother Cornbread, don't you know? Dat's Demosthenes Jones, de greatest banjo player what ever played. He is mute as a tree stump and twice as dumb, but he can play de banjar better than anyone!"*

"Not better than Bullfrog Johnson!"

"I says he can!" chimed in Burke.

"He can't!" Powell insisted.

We all started shouting at one another. Eagan, clearly steamed that he had been shouldered out of the way—I could not blame him—was the least enthusiastic of our line. Finally I waved my arms, saying, *"Silence! Quiet yo'selves! Dere is one way to find out for sure. Let him play us a banjo tune and den we'll see."*

Nods, vocal approval.

"Demosthenes!" I called.

Silence. I looked in his direction and saw Henry apparently asleep in his chair. He had improvised this comic twist on the spot, and the audience responded with laughter.

"DEMOSTHENES!" I shouted. *"Wake up befo' I come over dere and hit you wit dis old jawbone."*

Henry pretended to awaken with flailing movements, startled.

"Play us a song on de banjar so we can settle once for all who is de greatest banjar player in de land."

Henry rose to his feet and, milking the moment, shuffled slowly in his old-fashioned Sweeney costume, carrying the banjo to the front of the stage, wearing a frightened, cretinous expression. I have thought about that moment many times since. Looking out at the expectant crowd, he allowed his features to relax out of the idiotic expression and into one of complicity with the audience. Hefting the banjo into position, he began a very simple pattern, stroking down twice on a low string with his index fingernail, and then plucking once on the short, high string with his thumb, leaving the strings open. Then he fretted one note, keeping the pattern, then choking a string to create two notes out of one stroke. He brought this pattern up to speed, adding notes and beats until what he played became a cat's cradle of juggled rhythms. Then, with this machine spinning, out of the middle of it he brought, with all the rest of it going on simultaneously, a melody, which all recognized as "Massa's in de Cold, Cold Ground." But that song was usually sung as a lament; here it was set out in comic relief, its serious cadences mocked by the rhythmic filigree surrounding and teasing it. A voice from the audience exclaimed *"That ties it!"* and a swell of agreement rose as Henry lowered himself to one knee, still playing, raising the banjo up like a mother offering a child to a priest, then lowering it back to its normal position and rising once more to his feet, all the while still playing.

The hall erupted in shouts and applause. Finally Henry doubled the tempo, inserting a compact fireworks display of triplets, staggered rhythms, reversed patterns, and, on the last beat, raised the banjo as if it were a rifle, and in place of the final note *whacked* on the banjo's head with the flat of his hand as if he had fired the gun. Finished, he let his features slide back into uncomprehending vacancy as the audience rose as one, whistling, clapping, and stomping on the floor. Without acknowledging the crowd, Henry turned and shuffled back to his chair.

It took a full two minutes for the audience to begin to quiet down, and then only after Henry walked slowly back to the front of the stage and reprised the final part of his performance, this time sinking to both knees and bending backward before standing back up, playing all the while.

No individual number could follow this, of course, so we launched into the final ensemble number, "Clare de Kitchen," which did manage to rouse the audience, although every member was watching the unpredictable Demosthenes, seated once again at the rear, stage right, motionless, while the merriment went on in front. At the very last chorus, Henry shot to his feet and started dancing to the rhythm and playing banjo at the same time, and this pushed the crowd over the edge. When the curtain came down in front of us, we sat staring at it, stunned—I as much as any of us. Gilman came back and told us in great haste to do an encore. A sound like a stampede was making the curtain vibrate in ripples; the crowd was clearly beating on the very stage boards.

Hurriedly we regrouped, set ourselves, and the curtain rose as we launched into a reprise of "Clare de Kitchen" and the ungodly din grew even louder. The audience forced us to repeat this three times, and each time they would not stop until Henry gave out with a new dance.

When the crowd's appetite had finally been satisfied and the curtain stayed down, the members of the Virginia

Harmonists remained seated for a long minute or two, listening to the hubbub of conversation and footsteps out front as the audience made its way to the lobby. The general effect was that of having had a tornado rip through your house while you were eating dinner.

"Well," I said.

The fellows congratulated Juan García, and I translated. Henry sat, smiling and nodding and saluting the members. Only Mulligan kept silent, watching Henry closely. When he finally spoke, he did so without taking his eyes off of Henry.

"Some fucking Spaniard," Mulligan said. "Pure instinct. What's your real name, Juan?"

"Careful, Mulligan," I said. "These Mexicans are hot-blooded."

"Oh, rot," Mulligan said, standing up. "*Rot.* And that's no Spanish I've ever heard, either." He walked offstage.

I told the rest of the fellows that I would see them back at the dressing room. When they had left, I was about to speak to Henry in English, barely able to contain my excitement, when Gilman appeared, walking quickly toward us. "Well!" he said. "Well! You, sir, raised the devil himself tonight," heading straight for Henry to shake his hand. "You are a marvel."

"He doesn't speak English," I said.

"Oh, my. Well, I'm sorry. Bother English, then. Douglass—this man will be part of the show from now on, yes? Please assure me of this immediately. We very nearly had a riot. My Lord . . ." Turning to Henry again, he took Henry's hand and said, with genuine emotion, "My congratulations, you are a great artist. Please come back." He turned back to me. "Please."

"Yes," I said, "of course. Absolutely."

"Excellent, most excellent. A reporter was in the house to-night, by the way, Douglass. From the *Bee*. Let's see if we receive a notice." He didn't seem to know where to put himself. Indicating Henry, he said, "Please convey my admiration to him."

"Oh, I'm sure he gets the message," I said.

"By the way," the manager added, to me directly, "if Burke duns me for money again I'll cut off his balls and mail them back to his mother in her Galway whorehouse. Be kind enough to inform him."

"I will let him know," I said, cheerfully.

"Yes. Well . . ." Turning again to Henry, he said, "I hope we will see you tomorrow night."

Henry grinned back, nodded, and shook the manager's hand, and Gilman left the stage.

Henry removed his hat, which was soaked through. A line of lighter skin appeared across his forehead where the cork had come off. His expression was transcendent. "How was that?"

"How *was* it? Dear God. I don't see how we will be able to appear again without you. Mulligan is somewhat out of sorts—understandably, I'd say. But he will get over it. He's not really a bad fellow. Did you have all of that kneeling and what-not planned out?"

"No!" Henry said. "I thought of it right then." Now that it was over he could barely stand still with excitement.

"The falling-asleep was a touch of genius. All right," I said, "let's get ourselves out of here and repair to Dietmeyer's for a restorative. I have a feeling the Spanish masquerade will not have a long run, but we may as well maintain it as long as we can." I was beside myself. My gamble would pay the needed dividends; that was clear. We went our separate ways to clean up—myself to the dressing room, and Henry to Rose's workroom. Ten minutes later we walked out the service entrance, into the secret alley and, beyond it, the triumphal night.

PART
III

PART

III

8

Word of the new attraction at Barton's spread immediately. We were not able to add Henry to the official program until the following week because of a contract with a brother-and-sister singing team from Kreutbaden, ten-year-old twins with whose management—that is, their parents—we had signed a very Prussian contract. Our audiences made their impatience felt, and we had special posters printed up and notices placed, proclaiming the return of Demosthenes Jones on the next weekend.

There were logistical questions to work out. The problem of how to get Henry in and out of the theater with his banjo without drawing attention I partially solved by acquiring a second banjo for him that we would keep at Barton's. He would not leave his own banjo there; he liked playing it at night, he said, and practicing. We agreed, early on, that he would stop playing on the streets, as well. The possibility that someone might note a similarity between his street-corner prowess and the new sensation at Barton's was too much to risk.

Backstage, however, the masquerade began to unravel quickly. Mulligan, for his part, seemed to calm down a bit after Henry's second appearance. In fact, afterward I saw him place his hand on Henry's shoulder and say a few warm words. Henry forgot himself, smiled, and said "Thank you" in English. Eagan's misgivings, however, gave him, and me, no rest. A question here ("Why doesn't the fellow black up with us?"), a remark there ("Standoffish, isn't he?"), and it became clear that the others would need to be included in the masquerade. The risks in this were obvious, but it was unavoidable. So I called a meeting the week after Henry's second appearance, an extra hour before our usual arrival time. Henry would be a weekend attraction, exclusively, and this was a Tuesday.

At that meeting I told the basics of what I knew about Henry, and how I had encountered him. There was less surprise than I had anticipated, and more concern than I wanted. Burke asked about legal ramifications to our presenting a Negro, should the word somehow get out. I replied that we would be in a dubious situation if Henry's identity were generally known.

"Would we be shut down?" Powell asked.

"I am not certain," I replied, disingenuously. "But there is no question that we are running a risk, and I want to make sure that we are all agreed to continue as long as it seems sensible."

"If things are so dubious as they stand," Eagan said, "why are we taking this risk? Why don't we get rid of him now, before the audience comes to expect it without fail?"

"He's a great performer," Powell said.

"Isn't Mulligan more than enough of a banjo player?" Eagan said.

"That is not the question, Eagan," I said. "We have been in a hole. We've been drowning in yodelers and glass harmonica players, and our audiences have been dwindling. I assume you've noticed. And I assume you noticed the audience's reaction to Henry, and that you want the troupe to survive . . ."

I was about to add that our receipts had risen by approximately 30 percent in the past week alone, and every sign indicated that the trend would continue. But before I managed to get this out, to my great surprise, Mulligan jumped in, addressing Eagan.

"Michael," he said, "I will say this—the audiences love him. Even if there were something swampy about the law, the authorities cannot be unaware of his popularity. Barton certainly isn't. We have paid off city officials before, if I am not mistaken." I would not have expected Mulligan, of all of them, to rise in Henry's defense.

"Yes, well, do we know anything about him?" Eagan said, reddening. "He might be a criminal. He might be contraband . . ."

Both Powell and Mulligan jumped in with the obvious rejoinder that a fugitive from justice would hardly be likely to take refuge on a theater stage.

It came to a vote, and Mulligan led off with his strong support; Powell and Burke predictably followed him, and Eagan finally, and grudgingly, gave in, but not before leaving a muttered protest in his wake. "Mark my words: You are borrowing trouble."

Afterward I took Mulligan aside. "John," I said, "you surprised me in there."

"I like the fellow," he said. "And he is a real artist. I know you think I am fairly puffed-up on my own account, but someone who achieves his level of skill—one supports him. There is no competition there."

"Well . . ." I began.

"And Eagan is insufferable."

"He is, isn't he," I said.

Mulligan was pulling at his mustache. "But let's work up some type of number where we might both be featured. I would enjoy that."

Surprise, again. "I think that would be grand."

Absently, he repeated, "I'd like that very much."

Henry, for his part, was not slow to bring up the matter of the promised increase in his fee. After a considerable bit of wrestling we agreed that he would receive eight dollars for his next week's appearance. But he insisted that if he were to continue appearing he would have to receive ten dollars for each appearance.

"That is nearly what Mulligan makes," I said, before I thought better of it. "I won't hear of it."

"Mulligan does seven performances per week."

"Six," I replied. "And he is the cofounder. And anyway what of it?"

"We agreed that I need to stop playing on the street. Someone might realize I'm the same person." We had, indeed, already settled this point. "I can't survive on eight dollars a week."

"How much do you make on the street?" I said.

"Twenty dollars," he said, perfectly straight-faced.

I laughed, returned his stare, and said, "You ought to make your living playing cards. You have a strong enough stomach for a bluff!" To his credit, he laughed at this, and I went on: "If we add you for a second weekend night, and I think we will, I will pay you seven dollars and fifty cents per evening, for the two evenings."

He looked excited by this for a moment, before he remembered himself and summoned a doubtful look.

"You will be making fifteen dollars each week for two nights' work," I said, "instead of playing out on the street in all weather, with no guarantee of any income whatsoever."

He hemmed and he hawed, and I thought he must have Scots blood in him somewhere, but finally he agreed.

Thus did Henry Sims become a member, or an associate, of the Virginia Harmonists. To our songs and jokes, our foolery and whimsy, Henry added an edge of something else, a wildness—a vein of madness, even, or so it appeared to some—wedded to a brilliantly honed musical ability that seemed to ride the very edge of control. He was addicted to improvisation, and every night he threw something different into the mix, and it kept us off balance in a way that brought the performances to life.

If for months before his advent, we had struggled to remain a solid and reliable offering among many similar offerings, we were now once again the sensation of the town.

* * *

I cannot say that Henry and I became friends, exactly, but our rehearsals at my apartments became increasingly cordial—so much so that I allowed myself to wonder, now and again, where he had in fact come from, and who he was. I did not know, aside from a chance remark here and there, much of anything about my colleagues' innermost thoughts, or feelings—whether Mulligan felt lonely, or Burke speculated about the nature of the afterlife, or Powell kept letters from his first love. We agreed implicitly to keep our interactions confined to one plane only.

But in the weeks previous, Henry and I had shared such a sense of conspiratorial satisfaction that my ignorance about his background had begun to stand out in an odd relief. Although he was guarded in many ways, enigmatic, yet there was in him something that he kept alive, as if he had found some freedom for himself not only onstage but in life itself, and that spark brought out something in me, as well, part of which was an unaccustomed curiosity.

"Where did you learn to play music?" I asked. "Were your parents musicians?"

It was a fine afternoon, at my apartments, three weeks after his first appearance at the theater. I was already thinking of ways to broaden his participation in the program, and we had run through various scenarios. While rehearsing, we had played with a peculiar intensity and wordless communication; our understanding seemed perfect, even transcendent.

Why I chose that moment to ask him such a question, I am not sure. But I did.

He did not answer immediately, but finally he said, "No. Were yours?"

"My father played the violin," I said, "and those are my best memories of him."

"What's wrong with your other memories?"

I told him a bit about the mill, and then the farm, my brothers, the sheer boredom of it all. My father, and my mother, the disappointment inside her. He listened with an intense and, I believe, unfeigned interest.

"Is that why you don't play the violin?" he asked.

"I suppose so," I said.

"Do you never see your mother?" he said.

"No," I said.

"Do you miss her?"

"Yes," I said. "Where are your parents? You were not raised in Philadelphia."

"No," he said.

I waited for him to say more. He shifted restlessly on the divan, and then he started speaking. He told me he'd been raised "up north," near Boston. His family had a small farm, but his father died when Henry was quite young. His aunt lived with him and his mother, and they fared as well as they could, but they fell on hard times. Then a new man entered his mother's life and became his stepfather. Henry said he was used badly by this man, and was sent away to a boarding school. But it was a hard place, and when Henry returned home his stepfather, and his stepfather's sister, who sounded like quite a harridan, were so mean to him, and had driven such a wedge between himself and his beloved mother, that he resolved to run away, which he did.

I listened to it all with some astonishment. It was the stuff of novels, really. I had not been aware that boarding schools were available for Negroes.

"But where did you learn the banjo?" I asked. "How did you acquire your repertoire?"

"I lived with my uncle," he said. "He played with a circus, played all kinds of music. He showed me the banjo. He knew all the songs. I traveled with the circus."

"The circus!" I said. "I was on the road with Kimball's for years before I came here. What troupe were you with?"

He had a minor coughing fit, which alarmed me, but he recovered enough to say, "Nettles'."

I had not heard of them, but there were so many troupes that I did not wonder at it, and I had been out of that world for several years. I was going to ask him more about the troupe, but he preempted me by asking about the farm where I'd grown up. I told him a few more things, and I mentioned that I had changed my name, and that my family wouldn't have known how to find me if they'd wanted to. "I was born James MacDougall," I said. "I changed my name to Douglass when I joined the circus."

He raised himself on one elbow to look at me, and began laughing. I found this somewhat annoying, and I asked him why he found this funny. "Haven't you ever wanted to become someone other than you are?"

"I thought about it," he said, getting himself under control. "I was given a different name anyway."

"What do you mean?"

"The man my mother married," he said.

"You took his name?"

"Only for a while," he said.

I was not sure what he meant by that, but I didn't follow it up. Only later, as the weeks went by and we became more familiar, did I begin to allow myself to question the truth of his account.

I was spending more time at the theater during the days. With our popularity again in the ascendant, there was always correspondence, bills, production details, conferences with Birch on this or that bit of property deployment or stage construction. About half the time Rose would be there, working, and usually I would stop in and sit for a while with her, converse about this or that. I liked being in her workshop, where there was so much evident attention to detail, her process laid out like the insides of a clock. We would talk about nothing in particular during these visits—weather, or any scrap of news from the papers, events, what have you.

Every now and then I would insert a question to see if Rose would rise to the bait and offer some detail about her own life. One day, I asked where she had learned to sew so brilliantly and with such imagination. She was sewing at that moment, and she smiled and did not look up from her work.

"When I was a girl," she said, "I was kidnapped by a tribe of Zouaves and forced to sew saddlebags for their horses."

"Oh, now," I said. "There haven't been Zouaves in these parts for at least thirty years."

She laughed merrily, but she did not amend her story. Another time I asked her if she had always worn her hair short, and she told me she had had hair down to her ankles when she was a girl, but she had had to sell it to an upholsterer's in order to make ends meet. "They made some lovely pillows with it," she said.

I wondered if she joked that way with Eagan. I knew better, at least, than to ask her such a question.

One day I had spent the entire morning answering mail queries, after which I had gone out for lunch, leaving Rose there by herself. A lovely day, and not too hot. I walked all the way down to Front Street and had a meal at the Black Horse, for a change, then made my way back to Barton's. Inside, I heard voices coming from Rose's workroom, so I walked down to have a look.

To my surprise, I found Henry sitting on her couch. It was not an evening when Henry would be performing, and it was disorienting to see him there. My surprise must have registered on my face, because Rose laughed and said, "James, you look as if you've seen a ghost!"

"Not really," I said. "Is tea being served? What is the occasion?"

"I just stopped in to say hello," Henry said.

"Really!" I said.

"I have more free time now that I don't play on the street." He grinned, as if he had said something witty.

"I hope you made sure not to be seen coming in."

"I did," he said. "I'm good at that."

"Yes, you are," I said.

"I just now finished the outfits for 'Lucy Long,'" Rose said. This was a routine Powell and Burke had gotten up for the first half.

"Splendid," I said.

"Come in and sit with us," Rose said.

"I should not," I said. "I have receipts to tally up." Then, to Henry, "Be careful leaving."

Back in the dressing room, I was assailed by the most contradictory thoughts and feelings. As foolish as it seems, I was jealous. I had never been exactly jealous of Rose's arrangement with Eagan. Dismayed, yes, but not jealous, as I was quite sure she did not love him. There was no reason to think anything left-handed was going on with Henry, of course, and yet his presence there felt like an intrusion into the order of things. And, beyond that, there was a recklessness in it. With all the effort we expended to insulate Henry from suspicion, this seemed to show bad judgment at the least. I stewed over it as my receipts sat moldering on the dressing table.

Perhaps five minutes later, Henry appeared at the door. "You left so fast," he said. "Why didn't you come in?"

"Listen," I said, motioning for him to step in and close the door behind him, "be careful spending time with Rose. Eagan is a jealous type, and we don't want him getting the wrong idea."

"Did I do something wrong?"

"No!" I said. "Of course not. Just remember that we could be fined or closed down if word got out to the public that you're not one of us."

He narrowed his eyes as if he were trying to discern some underlying meaning to what I had said, and I saw that I had hurt his feelings.

"I'm just saying to keep alert, is all," I said. "For everyone's sake."

"I stay alert," he said. "I'm always alert."

"Yes," I said. "I know that."

We exchanged a few more awkward phrases, and then he left.

I had no basis for any odd feelings whatsoever, and I did my best to ignore them as they swarmed. But I soon had something much larger to worry about.

On Thursday afternoon I was at the theater, sifting through paperwork, when I heard a knocking from the general direction of the stage door. I ignored it at first, but as it persisted, I got up to see who it was. The box office was open, out front, so I had no idea who this might be.

When I got there I saw a figure standing at the door who sent a chill through me. Tall, dressed rather crudely, thin, with a cotton eye turned out perhaps thirty degrees to the side. He wore a hideous brimmed hat made of some sort of oily-looking leather.

I asked how I might help him.

He said, "I'd like to speak to the proprietor, if I might."

"Did you inquire at the box office? The theater isn't open yet."

"Yeah," he said, smiling slightly. "They told me to come around back here."

"What does this concern?"

"Are you the proprietor?"

"I am the manager of the Virginia Harmonists," I said.

"That's all right," he said. He had an unpleasant smile, a kind of sneer that curled his upper lip. "Can I come in?"

I had absolutely no reason, nor desire, to invite this man inside, and I said, "I am in the middle of working at the moment. Please state your business."

"Sure," he said. "I've been hired to find and return contraband, ran off from Virginia. He's a musician and I'm checking with theaters to see if they might know anything."

"Negroes aren't allowed onstage in Philadelphia."

"Yeah," he said, chuckling as if I had said something amusing. "I know that. But I figured maybe he'd want to be around theaters. So nobody has turned up looking for work?"

"No," I said.

The man squinted at me, with that curled-lip smile. "You sure about that?"

"I imagine that I am quite sure."

"Oh, all right. I was just checking. You looked like you might not have been too sure. This fellow's light-skinned, green eyes, plays the banjo. His owner says he's smart and thinks he's as good as a white man. Somebody taught him to read. His name was Joseph, but he probably changed it."

It took all my will to keep my face a blank.

"No?" he said, again, looking at me as if reading fine print. "Well, if you talk to anybody who does, or if you hear anything, you can get a message to me here." He gave me a card with a handwritten address of a rooming house on Eighth Street.

"Certainly," I said.

"Hey," he said, "I heard you have the best nigger show in town. I'm going to see it before I leave."

I tried to locate an appropriate response. "That is fine," I said. Then, I asked, "When do you leave?"

"That's still kind of up in the air," he said. "It depends on how quickly I find the boy."

"Of course," I said.

He nodded, still looking at me, with a slight squint, then he left.

I shut the stage door and walked to the dressing room.

Once there, I sat down, nearly overcome. For a few moments I was certain that I would be sick to my stomach, and I lay my head on the dressing table.

I had no way of getting word to Henry; I would not see him until the next evening's performance. Why had he not proceeded to Canada if he was in such jeopardy? Wouldn't it have been natural to assume that his owner would send someone to find him? I was stunned by the recklessness of his deception. And he had lied to me.

Later that evening, Thursday, I began my preparations, amongst my colleagues, for the show, but my mind was on fire. As they joked and gossiped, I spread the cork across my forehead and down my cheeks, smoothing it, evening out the opaque coat.

I was born neither blind nor stupid. I knew that the Negroes we depicted so fancifully were, in real life, subject to harsh treatment and compulsory labor. And worse. I knew it, yet the images of Negroes that we summoned represented such a release from oppressive fact that they had become a necessity, for ourselves and for our audience. I had let myself be deceived, though I should have known better. And now, from behind that beautiful, pernicious illusion, reality had come snarling.

It was one thing to dare convention by presenting a Negro in disguise. It was another to harbor a fugitive and to conceal him from his owner's agent. Such an act had legal ramifications that far surpassed those implicit in simply presenting a Negro. He had put not only himself at risk, but all of us. What, exactly, did I owe him now—this brilliant illusionist and vital presence, this reckless liar and manipulator, who had used me and placed our troupe at risk?

And, yes, whom I had used, and manipulated, as well.

Sitting at the dressing table, besieged by these questions, I caught my reflection in the mirror, staring back at me from behind its black mask. What did I owe, and to whom?

9

Rooming house off Sansom on Eighth Street. Dust motes in the stale air. The wash basin, chipped porcelain, the pitcher inside. The green chenille bedspread on the single bed, bowed down in the middle, and a framed print of a cat on the wall. The faded hooked rug a small island on the worn wood floor.

He hated cities. He had been in Philadelphia for most of a week and had turned up nothing. It had been four days' riding to get there. He had spent the last night before his arrival at the Warfield farm, ten miles out of town to the west. From Warfield's city directory, he made a list of furniture makers and dealers, as well as music stores. He had included theaters as well; a boy interested in music might get a cleanup job in one of them, just to be around it. The riverfront saloons were likely places if the boy were playing on the street. The main police station was in the City Hall, at Chestnut and Fifth, although police were, in his experience, useless. What they called Darktown was in the south part of the city, around Lombard and Sixth, seeping out westward. That would be his final stop, only if nothing else panned out.

Slaves, he liked to say, thought in fragments. They had no idea of the big patterns. They saw things in flashes. They had no conception of the future. What future did they have to plan for? It was given to the white man to see the larger picture. He had formed an image of this Joseph as a spoiled boy who liked attention, who thought anything was possible because Master was his daddy. Tull's specialty was foreclosing possibility.

His first stop, four days earlier, had been the police headquarters, a large, barely furnished room in City Hall, sun pouring in through high windows and across the varnished wood floor, a single desk on the left side and one on the right, facing each other. At the nearer of the two, a man with sandy hair and sideburns, eating an apple. Opposite, a black-haired fellow with a low forehead, clean-shaven, every few seconds tossing a cherry pit across the room at the other. On a bench at the far end, a plump man, wearing a squat black hat with a narrow, shiny brim—a ridiculous-looking hat—speaking to the room at large, while its occupants ignored him.

"You could put a ferry boat farther south on the Delaware. My cousin was a ferry boat man, made good money doing it. They have a beef brisket now at Dodge's, but you have to buy a pint. Beef brisket causes goiter, but I'd take the chance. The gravy runs out of it; I saw one of those turnbottoms lick it off the side of the dish. Right off the side of the dish . . ."

Tull stood inside the doorway, waiting for someone to acknowledge him. The man on the bench did not break stride in his commentary, but shifted his attention to Tull.

"Now there's a man looks exactly like my cousin Alfred. Alfred had a perfectly good job at a countinghouse, but he couldn't find a wife. Now there is a hat. That's leather. A milliner on Twelfth Street will make a hat out of any material whatever . . ."

The sandy-haired man finished his apple and, still impassive, tossed the core at his tormentor across the room. It struck the wall behind the other man. Finally, he addressed Tull without looking at him.

"What do you need?"

"Are you an officer of the law?" Tull said.

The man looked at him flatly. "I am."

Tull offered a disingenuous smile, his lip curling up slightly on the left side. "Sorry, officer. It was a little hard to tell." He stated the reason for his visit, gave the boy's name.

"Most of them don't keep their names," the sandy-haired officer said. "You took out ads, I suppose?"

"His owner did. This one plays the banjar."

"Lot of them out there." To the black-haired man at the desk across the room, he said, "Didn't you say you saw one the other day?"

The cherry thrower said, "It was a fiddler." To Tull, he said, "You want a fiddler?"

Tull felt contempt starting up in himself, like a muscle cramp.

The man with the ridiculous hat, who had kept up his commentary during these exchanges, said, "There's a jig plays banjo and dances in the square. I can show you."

The sandy-haired man said, "They'll play in the parks, or down by the docks. Outside the saloons. Niggertown is down on Lombard Street."

Tull asked if there were police available to help should he need it.

Sandy hair shrugged and said, "It'd have to go before a magistrate." He looked Tull up and down. "We've got our own responsibilities."

The cherry thrower chimed in, "He's the captain. What he says goes. If you want to find the Schuylkill Rangers, we'll put up a nice headstone for you." Laughed like a schoolboy.

"I believe it's the law," Tull said, "that any citizen is compelled to help capture a runaway slave. Even a policeman."

The captain regarded Tull. "Is that the law? Thank you. We don't have problems with the Colored here, as long as they don't cause trouble."

"It's the Irish," the cherry thrower said. "And the rest of the Papal refugees."

"You can hire out Trogdon," the captain said. "He's available at a reasonable hourly rate."

Tull looked at the doughy man, who brightened instantly.

"Don't forget your hat," the cherry thrower said.

They walked through the sun and dappled shade, a beautiful day for most people.

"They make fun of me wearing the hat, but one day we'll have uniforms. Hizzoner says so. Where do you come from? Do they get the police up well there? I'm interested to know. I wasn't born in Philadelphia, but I say if I'm here I'll do my best. Are you planning on staying in town?"

On and on it went, as they approached the square. He had offered this Trogdon a dollar to come with him, and another two if it was the right man and they took him. Now he was sorry. The boy wouldn't perform so near the police head-quarters. Trogdon was going on about a show he had seen somewhere, the minstrels this and that . . .

"I love a nigger show," the half-wit was saying. "The best is at Barton's. They have a new fellow plays the banjo kneeling down. I saw it the other night. Best in town." He began sing-ing: "*De boatman dance, de boatman sing . . .*"

"Be quiet," Tull said.

"He's over there," his companion said, now, pointing across the square to a small group of people watching a Negro dance. Even from across the square, Tull knew that this was not the boy he was looking for. Face blue-black, and thirty years old, easily.

"Is that your man?" Trogdon asked.

"No," Tull said. "This is the only one?"

"Well . . ." the fool looked around anxiously. "There are plenty. But whyn't we get him anyway?"

Tull reached into his pocket and withdrew some coins. "Here," he said.

The police put out his hand and took the coins, spreading them on his palm to count. Tull started away.

"Here," the police said. "I can find more."

"I know where you are if I need you," Tull said, walking off.

The sun cast deep shade under the street awnings, the hanging signs clamoring for attention, like beggars asking for handouts. It pressed down upon the construction, the wooden board fences along the building sites, bleached the posters and flyers for theatrical presentations. Impersonators, actors, illusionists, runaways, fly-by-nights. The city was full of trap doors and tunnels, and pedestrians clogged the street. The cart horses had made plenty of mess, and the smell was powerful. Even shit smelled worse in the city than it did in the country.

Two blocks north of Market, a showroom. Tull asked a young man with thinning hair and a long beard if he hired people to do piecework.

The shop man shook his head and said, "No, friend. We have no need for any aid along those lines. The docks are your best chance, I'd say."

"I didn't mean for me," Tull said. "I'm looking for someone who might have done some woodwork part-time. Any of the makers around here hire people like that sometimes?"

"No," the man said. "Generally we train people and keep them around. A good turner you don't let go, you know. You might try the dealers down on South Street. They hire part-timers, delivery men."

Near Callowhill on Second Street, a banjo in the window of a chair maker's shop.

A cluttered but orderly space that smelled heavily of varnish and sawed wood. A red-haired man in middle age, using a rasp on a chair leg, set the rasp down, asked if he could help him.

"I saw that banjar you got in your window," Tull said. "You selling that?"

"The one in the window, no. That was one I made for a lark. You play the banjo, you're welcome to play it. I wouldn't sell it."

"You ever get folks asking about it?"

"Oh, once in a while, you know. Especially with the river men—they sometimes play a banjar. I had a Colored fellow came in and played it once. People were surprised I let him come in and play it. I said he had as much right to play it as anyone."

"What did he look like?"

The man frowned. "What do you mean?"

"I'm looking for a Colored fellow who plays banjo. Light-skinned, about so tall. Green eyes."

The furniture man found a spot of interest on the arm of a nearby chair, and ran his hand over it twice. Without looking up, he said, "You're hunting contraband?"

"I've been hired to retrieve property."

The furniture man nodded but said nothing, brushed off the chair one more time.

"You can leave now," he said.

"Well, just a minute, there, friend . . ."

The man's face mottled red. "You're nobody's friend. Get out."

Tull made a note of the address before walking off down the street.

* * *

The barkeep at Dwyer's Saloon set out cheese and crackers. Across the street, Boone Wharf sat cracking in the sun.

"We got in some nice oysters, out of Baltimore," he said. "This is about the last of them until October."

"I'm fine with the cheese, thanks."

"Suit yourself."

"Hey, any jig musicians around? I was told there were some good ones down around here. One plays the banjo."

"They come and they go. Out hunting, are you?"

That was pretty quick, Tull thought. "I enjoy music," he said.

The bartender kept wiping glasses, unsmiling.

"There's more fiddle players than banjo," he said. "One banjo player down by the Black Horse now and then."

"He a good one?"

"I don't pay much attention to it," the barkeep said, putting up the glasses. "He always has a crowd, though."

"What's he look like?"

The bartender shrugged.

"Real dark nigger?" Tull said.

The bartender gave him a quick, hard look. "I didn't get close to him. Dark? No—not so dark. The little I saw, he could have been a Mexican. You want another cider?"

Tull felt a percolation commence in his chest.

"Where's the Black Horse?"

The bartender removed the glass from in front of Tull and drew more cider from a small barrel at the end of the bar. He came back, set the glass down, and said, "That's two cents. Two blocks up. You'll see it. There's a monkey painted on the side."

Tull placed a coin on the bar and walked out the front door.

Two blocks away he saw the sign advertising Bigelow's Bitters, customers entering and leaving the Black Horse. It was getting on toward lunchtime. Tull walked in. The interior was dark after the street, but light trickled in from the front windows, which were bayed out under a sidewalk canopy. Five or six men at the bar, another half dozen at tables. Tull moved through the room and found an opening halfway down. When the bartender approached, he ordered a phosphate and asked when the jig banjo player showed up.

"Hasn't been around for a couple weeks," the bartender said. "I wish he'd come back. He was good for business."

"Doesn't look like you're suffering," Tull said, all fellowship.

"This is nothing," the bartender said. "You'd have people outside like it was the circus. Made them thirsty. That's a penny."

Tull set a coin down on the bar. "I heard about him. Kind of light-complected, like a Mexican?"

"That's him."

"Is his name Joseph?" Tull said.

"I don't know what his name is." The bartender looked at Tull for a moment. "Where are you from?"

"St. Louis," Tull said, smiling.

The bartender took the coin and walked away.

Tull sipped from his glass. Across the bar, behind the risers of bottles, he gazed back at himself from the mirror. He liked knowing things that other people did not know. He smiled raffishly at his reflection. He summoned a menacing look, squinted. He raised one eyebrow, turned his head slightly to one side, held his own gaze. He let his features slump into a vacant, idiotic expression. He laughed out loud. The bartender looked down the bar at him. He sipped from the glass. It was not good, however, that the boy hadn't been seen for weeks. Maybe he had gone on to Canada, the way they liked them to. If the boy was gone, he was gone; not much he could do about that. He stared at himself in the glass, finished the last of his beverage, and called the barkeep over. He took one of his cards—a simple white slip on which he had penciled the address of the rooming house—and slid it to the bartender, with a ten-cent piece.

"I'm staying here," Tull said. "If that banjo player shows up send a messenger to me as quick as you can, and it will be five dollars for you."

The barkeep looked down at the card without touching it, then he slid the coin off and put it in his pocket and placed the card next to the coin box behind him and moved down the bar to another customer.

Tull stood at the top of Market Street, looking out toward the river. He turned from the river and looked down Market into Philadelphia, with its jabbering sidewalks and stalls, its parks and columned buildings, and the great, blind, presiding eye of the City Hall tower. The wagons, the blistering sun, the awning shade, the signs. He exhaled slowly, making a hissing sound with his tongue against his front teeth. "Come here, Joseph," he thought. "Come to me."

* * *

He visited a dozen furniture makers, and at least as many saloons, a handful of music stores and six theaters, and by Thursday afternoon he knew nothing more than that a Mexican-looking banjo player had worked outside the Black Horse and had not been seen for several weeks. No messages had come to the rooming house. None of the furniture makers had employed the boy, or they wouldn't admit to it if they had. None of the music stores knew about him, none of the theaters knew about him. The boy, he admitted, might very well have left town. If he had ever been there in the first place.

He had saved Lombard Street for last. Word of a white man looking for someone would spread around Darktown faster than you could sneeze. And Tull did not like being outnumbered by free blacks, hostile to his mission and accountable to no one. Lombard was a last resort.

Against his inclination, he had returned to police headquarters after a Thursday morning round of theaters, to ask for a competent deputy, or two, who could accompany him. He arrived to find the same trio of officers occupying the same positions in which he had found them four days previous.

"Would you like an apple?" the captain said.

Trogdon, wearing his shiny-brimmed hat, was speaking to the black-haired officer, who had leaned back against the wall in his chair, with his eyes closed.

"I wouldn't eat the stuff," Trogdon was saying. "Beets give you gas, and they say it gives a dog the distemper. I wouldn't want to find out. They say you need to drink water, but if you drink it out of a public tap you get maggots."

"Especially if you're a dog," the black-haired man said.

"I need two deputies," Tull said.

"I wouldn't know about a dog," Trogdon said. "I've never seen a dog with the maggots. Hullo—have you found the nigger?"

"You'll need a warrant," the captain said.

"A warrant?" Tull said. He stared at the captain. "This is a niggertown search. What do I need a warrant for?"

The captain shrugged. "That's the law. The magistrate is on the second floor. Shouldn't take more than an hour, maybe two."

To Trogdon, Tull said, "You want to make five dollars?"

"I have a friend could help us," Trogdon said, outside on the sidewalk. "You said *deputies*—I heard that. He would not mind making a dollar. He lives nearby."

"Where?"

"Just the other side of Cherry Street," Trogdon said, already out of breath trying to keep up with Tull. "In the Excelsior."

Cherry was four blocks in the wrong direction.

"You're sure he's there?"

"Oh, he's always there," Trogdon said, breathing hard as they walked. "He's a good man, if you need one. He's done every kind of work except for beekeeping. He has never kept bees, never would. Hates them. I do, as well. Most insects are an annoyance. They make maggots . . ."

At the corner of Cherry Street, Trogdon looked around, apparently puzzled, and after a moment said, "Oh, two more blocks."

The Excelsior was a flophouse on the other side of Vine Street. The hallway smelled of mold and urine.

"This one here," Trogdon said, boldly leading the way.

The door was open into a room where a man lay on a bed, reclining, smoking a pipe.

"Hallo, Vic!" Trogdon said. The man looked up at him. "Where's the parrot?" To Tull, he said, "Vic has a parrot with the most extraordinary . . ."

"Shut up," Tull said. To the reclining man, he said, "Can you stand up?"

"I can," the man said.

"I'll give you three dollars if you'll come with us for a couple hours."

"Well . . . what . . ." the man began.

"Police business!" Trogdon said.

"Can you keep your mouth shut and walk around?"

"Well," the man said, frowning, "I . . . yes." He slid himself forward on the bed and stood up, leaned over and began emptying his pipe to refill it. Concentrating on the pipe, the man said, "That is quite an interesting hat."

Tull grabbed him by the shoulder. A thin trickle of drool made its way through the man's stubble.

"Leave your pipe."

The trio walked the ten blocks to Lombard Street through the hot afternoon, across the tracks. The neighborhood changed like a change of weather, turned shabbier, except for a huge stone church at the corner, a block away. Isolated brick houses sat amid rough wooden shacks and sheds. The people on the street, almost all of them black, walked along, seemingly without any destination. Blacks in proper jackets, blacks in rags, young blacks, old blacks. Tull felt disgust at the disorder of it all. At Fourth Street, a Negro with a patch of discolored skin on his forehead sat on a wooden crate, holding a violin.

"There!" Trogdon cried. "Why not collar him?"

"He's looking for a banjo player," his friend said. "What's wrong with you?"

A couple of Negroes walked past, looked at them.

Tull approached the old man. He might, Tull thought, know a banjo player if there were money behind the question. Trogdon started to say something, but his friend slapped his arm lightly to quiet him.

"Uncle," Tull said to the man, "play me a song."

"You my nephew?" the man said. There was something wrong with him, Tull saw now. Something in the eyes.

"Figure of speech," Tull said. "Play me a song and I'll give you a nickel."

"You play me a song and I'll give you a dime."

Tull nodded, started to move away. His instincts were off.

"Next time bring a dollar," the Negro called after him.

Two more blocks and they paused again. Tull looked up and down the street. Absently, he said, "Do either of you spend time down here?"

"I wouldn't," Trogdon said.

"Where would you stay if you were a nigger just came to town?"

Trogdon's friend, Vic, said, "There's a place on the other side of Seventh Street."

Tull had avoided looking closely at this Vic, but now he did. The man wore a graying blond mustache on a lip nudged forward by too-prominent upper teeth; a bead of moisture hung, glistening, at the tip of his nose.

"What kind of place?" Tull said.

"It's sort of a rooming house, or a warren."

"How do you know about this place?"

"Ha!" Trogdon said. "Vic's a ladies' man!"

"Oh shut up, would you please?" Vic said. "All he ever does is talk, have you noticed?"

Tull looked the man in the eyes.

"It's like a chicken coop," Vic said. "Or . . . a kennel! A kennel for humans!"

"Show me," Tull said.

Just past Seventh, on the south side of Lombard, a walkway between two modest wood-frame houses. Down the street two colored girls were playing skip-rope, one of them singing, "*Last night, the night before, twenty-four robbers at my door . . .*"

"It's through there," Trogdon's friend said. "I don't know that I want to go in."

"Then go stand across the street," Tull said.

"Can I sit on those steps?" he said.

"I don't care what you do. Stay there, and if you see anybody carrying a banjo, come inside and get me."

The man looked around nervously.

"You scared of a few niggers?"

"I didn't say that. I did not say I was afraid."

"You want your three dollars?"

"Of course I do."

Tull started across the street. To Trogdon, he said, "You come with me."

Trogdon's head was shaking as if he had the palsy.

"I'm glad of that," Trogdon said, as they walked back across the street. "I wouldn't much like sitting out here by myself. I had an uncle wrestled a nigger one time at a lumber camp and the nigger turned into a panther. This was before he met his wife. She was no good at all. Goats used to graze all up by Germantown . . ."

"All you need to do is wear your hat and sit still," Tull said. "You'll get two dollars if you can do that much."

"Two?" Trogdon said. "I thought it was five."

"You'll get five if we find him and take him."

Tull and Trogdon made their way down the narrow passage to a courtyard where something was cooking in a large pot suspended over a fire. A lone Negro sat on a bench, looking as if he had just come off of a prodigious drunk. Red eyes, and his shoulders in a slouch. Nobody else around as far as Tull could make out. The courtyard was open to the sky, where it was still early afternoon among the sparse clouds.

"How are you today?" Tull said.

Barely looking up, the man said, "Still a nigger."

Tull chuckled appreciatively. "I got two dollars for somebody'll tell me where I can find a fellow plays the banjo."

Looking up now at Tull and squinting, as if to focus, the Negro said, "We got a banjo player here. *Good* banjo player. He not in now, though."

"Brownskin?"

The red-eyed man frowned slightly. "Light-complected."

"Green eyes?"

"I never got that close to him. Eyes like a girl. Where the money?"

"Get up," Tull said. The man stood. To Trogdon, Tull said, "Sit down there." Trogdon did so, looking nervously around the courtyard.

"People coming in here giving orders," the red-eyed man said.

A woman's voice yelled out, "Jerome, get in your room." The woman attached to the voice appeared out of one of several little hallways that led into the courtyard. "Get in your God damn room," she repeated. Then, to Tull: "Who are you?"

"Stay where you are," Tull said to Jerome. Then, "Just a friend of music, ma'am," all politeness. He saw the woman look at his hat and frown. "He said you have a banjo player living here?"

"Who you coming around here asking questions?"

"Well," he said, "I got five dollars here if I can get some help finding this fellow, kind of light-complected, just like he said, plays the banjar . . ." He saw her eyes widen briefly, and this told him all he needed to know. He had raised the price somewhat in honor of her apparent rank. "You know any-body like that?"

"Why you want to pay five dollars? That's a lot of money for white trash like you."

He started toward her.

"You keep coming at me and I'll cut you into ribbons, man," the woman said. She had whipped out a long straight razor from somewhere. Tull stopped. "I'll cut out that white eye of yours. You like that?"

Trogdon sat on the bench watching, his head trembling,

and did not move. Tull forced a smile. "You have that boy here, we will get him and we will take you in along with him. For protecting a fugitive. Maybe you sell a little cooch on the side, too? You'll be lucky if they don't chop off those tired-out titties of yours."

She laughed in his face. "I don't know who you're talking about plays the banjo. I like to see them try come here and pick up somebody. I'd like to see that."

"The law says you're going to be arrested and locked up. You like to see that?" he said. Watching her closely, he added, "I'll give you ten dollars."

"Don't talk to me about the law. Them police about the sorriest white men I ever saw. Like your friend there. I take care of them, anyway. No police come around here. Go on get out of here before I blow my whistle and they put you on the cooling board."

To the red-eyed man, Tull said, "Where does the banjo player stay?"

"Down the hall there," the man said. "Door with the yellow on it."

"I don't want to hear that either of you moved or said a word," Tull said.

"Here—" Trogdon began.

"Shoot them if they move," Tull said.

Tull drew his pistol and walked toward the nearest of the three passageways that led out of the courtyard. It was very dark and narrow, the only light that which struggled in from the courtyard, behind him. It smelled dank and vegetal. He walked slowly, letting his eyes adjust to the rapidly thickening gloom. A doorway, on his right, painted blue. The outlines of another doorway took shape, on his left. Squinting, Tull made out a faint yellowish tint amid the gray gradations of the remaining light. The door, a plank on rude hinges, was secured from outside with a hook and eyelet. The occupant, whoever it was, could not be inside. Tull unhooked the latch.

A small room, perhaps ten feet square, dim light filtering in through a shuttered window. Tull made out that it was lined with wood, like a ship's cabin. Drawers, shelves, cubbyholes. A pallet on a low platform took up half the space; a pair of very fine hunting boots sat on the floor. On the pallet were some folded clothes—a shirt, some breeches. And a banjo.

He sat down on the pallet and picked up the instrument. It was identical to the one he had seen in the wood shop at The Tides, right down to the carving at the top. There was nothing to do, now, until the boy got back. But the situation was a puzzle. The boy could be warned off easily. If they posted themselves on the street they would attract attention, and if they remained inside someone could warn the boy away before they ever saw him. He was too close, now, to make any misstep. He lay the instrument back on the pallet and quit the room, latching the door.

Outside, on Lombard Street, Vic sat on the steps of a building, leaning against the stair casing, his eyes half shut, staring straight ahead while two children stood a ways off, eyeing him and giggling. Tull approached.

"This is tedious," Vic said.

"You said you've been here before, right?"

"Once or twice."

"Are there other ways in and out?"

"Pardon me?" Vic said, archly.

"Entrances."

"I imagine," Vic said. "The place is full of little tunnels. It's like an anthill."

Tull looked down Lombard Street, trying to sift through the human traffic as it walked, multiplied by shadows that were just beginning their slide toward evening. The fellow was useless sitting out there, but he was not particularly conspicuous. Still, someone might take notice. But Tull did not want him inside, chattering with his friend.

"How long must we stay here?" Vic said.

Tull started across the street. "I'll be back," he said.

He walked west on Lombard past three identical two-story brick houses to the corner of Eighth Street, then turned left. Past a series of three low wooden buildings, barely more than lean-tos, separated by narrow passageways. On the sidewalks along the way, Negroes sat on barrels, stood arguing by the curb. Three of them had set up a board on a crate and were playing dominoes. A one-story brick house with stairs leading down into a basement passage. No one appeared to take any notice of him. At the end of the block he turned left on South Street and made his way alongside a wall of wooden planking that stretched for a third of the block, set onto some kind of masonry footing, finally giving out at the edge of a series of sheds. Then a small brick stable that went to the corner of Seventh, where Tull turned left again and made his way back to Lombard. The fool was right about that much, at least. The place was a sieve. No way to monitor every entrance.

* * *

Three hours passed. Shadows seeped across the courtyard, like ink across a blotter. Trogdon sat on the bench, talking to the red-eyed man, who was asleep, or pretending to be asleep. There was no sign of the woman. The pot of cooking food had disappeared.

Tull could not escape the feeling that the moment was slipping through his hands and he was helpless to stop it. If he walked outside, he was conspicuous. If he stayed inside, he was at the mercy of anyone outside who could warn the boy. On Lombard, long shadows on the pavement. Trogdon's friend was asleep the third time Tull went out.

"How long must we stay here?" the man, Vic, asked.

"Till he comes back," Tull said, looking up and down the street.

"Let me at least come inside with the two of you."

"I thought you didn't want to go in."

"Now I do."

Two young women entered the courtyard, regarded Tull and his companions with questioning eyes, seemed to come to a quick decision, disappeared down two different hallways. A man with a withered arm walked in, looked at the trio of strangers, and went off down a hallway. A large man in work clothes appeared, looked at them unafraid, and sat down on a bench opposite the red-eyed man, to whom he made an inquiry with a subtle facial expression. The red-eyed man shook his head, barely noticeably. The bigger man pulled a small peach out of his pocket and ate it. When he had finished, he threw the pit onto the remains of the fire in the middle of the courtyard and walked back outside.

Night coming on, and Tull ran through his options. This

was the city, he thought. Gangs of menacing Negroes, countless hiding places for criminals, ineffectual law enforcement,
men who would not last ten minutes if they had to survive in
the country. The courtyard was ominously quiet. Even Trogdon had shut up. The situation could turn bad very easily,
and Tull knew it. The woman with whom he had had his
encounter had not returned.

Tull went back down the passageway and examined the
boy's door and latch. Not surprisingly, the fit was inexact. He
stepped inside, shut the door, took out his knife and, sliding
the blade between the door's edge and the jamb, lifted the
hook with the tip of the knife. It took three tries, but he was
able to drop the hook into the eyelet on the jamb, and then
unhook it again, from inside. Someone could stay inside and
the boy would return and think that no one was there. The
boy had to come back sometime. The three of them could
stay in the room, and wait.

But the odds were overwhelming that the boy had already
been warned off. And, if he hadn't, he would be. Niggertown
was a spiderweb; touch it in one place and the whole thing
vibrated. It had been a mistake to leave that fool outside, even
across the street, looking like a frightened animal. A mistake
to leave the jabbering fool in the courtyard. A mistake to
bring them to begin with. Now he knew the boy was in the
city. They had found his nest, and the idea that he might have
slipped away infuriated Tull.

In the courtyard, he got Trogdon and his friend together
and quietly offered them three dollars apiece if they would
remain there with him, overnight if necessary, until the boy
arrived. Tull knew it was pointless, and he didn't want to do

it, and he knew they wouldn't, but he wanted to hear them say it.

"I don't value my life at such a bargain," Vic said.

"They perch like vultures," Trogdon said. "Have you seen a vulture pull the entrails out of a squirrel? They put one of their claws on the neck and they pull at the entrails. They pull, as if you had snagged something with a fishing line. That's a thing to avoid. I had a cousin crippled that way, trying to boat a submerged cannon . . ."

Tull looked up at the sky above the courtyard, sugared and smeared with pinks and purples, banked-up clouds backlit by the last of the lurid sun. The voluptuous beauty mocked him. Spending the night there, alone, dark passageways teeming with unbroken city Negroes . . . There were too many places to hide in the city, too many ways of covering your tracks, too many do-gooders to help, to keep an eye out, to warn the boy off. It disgusted him. He wanted to hit something. He turned away and left the courtyard abruptly, headed down the passageway to Lombard Street.

"Wait!" Trogdon called. The two men hurried after him.

Tull was on the sidewalk just outside the passageway in the darkening evening. He would keep the advance, as agreed upon, and return without the boy. He had bought a ticket for the minstrels on Arch Street the next evening, Friday. He would spend one more day of Stephens's expense money, see if anyone got a message to him at the rooming house, take in the show, then get out on Saturday morning. He could get that much out of the trip to this sewer, at least.

"Where should we go now?" Trogdon said.

"You can go and stick your hat up your ass and set it on fire for all I care," Tull said.

He drew a money pouch out of his jacket pocket, opened it, and felt the men press close, greedy.

"This was quite a fiasco," Vic said.

"Here," Tull said, ignoring him, looking down at the transaction. To Trogdon, he gave the agreed-upon two dollars.

"I should think we might get more, given how long we spent," Trogdon said, counting the coins, his head shaking.

Ignoring him as well, Tull put two dollars in the other's hand. Vic counted the coins.

"I thought we had agreed on three dollars as my fee," he said.

Tull looked at the man, now, standing in front of him with his hand still out, the coins on his palm, looking at Tull with a mixture of fear, indignation, and irony. A weak man with a vein of effrontery in him. He probably enjoyed taking punishment, Tull thought.

"You fell asleep," Tull said.

"I don't wonder," the man said. "I had nothing to do but sit there."

"Then you're lucky to get that."

The man looked at the coins in his hand.

Trogdon was watching Tull. "Come on, Vic," he said. "I'm satisfied."

"Well, I'm not," Vic said.

"You'd better be," Tull said. "Get out of here now."

The man assumed a wounded expression. "You needn't speak crossly to me," he said.

Tull pulled his pistol out of his jacket. The man looked at Tull as if this might be a joke. Tull rapped the man's hand with the barrel and sent the coins tumbling to the sidewalk.

"The niggers can have the money if you don't want it," Tull said.

"That was unnecessary," Vic said, crouching down to get the coins.

"Was it?" Tull said. He cuffed the back of the figure's head with the gun barrel, and Vic fell forward on one knee and put up his left hand to fend off any other blows.

"Stop it," he said. "Vicious bastard."

Tull laughed out loud at this. It was funny, as if a mouse had addressed him in a booming voice. He slammed the side of the man's head and sent him pitching forward onto the sidewalk. The man rolled to his back and looked up at Tull, panicked. This was correct, Tull thought. Now we were getting somewhere. He pointed the gun at the man's face and knelt with one knee upon his chest.

"Don't move, Vic," he said, smiling.

"Help!" the man called out. "Help!"

Now Tull laughed again, and he used the butt of the gun to break the man's front teeth off into his mouth. A spatter of blood appeared on Tull's knee. The man was crying.

"You got my pants dirty," Tull said.

"Here," Trogdon said. "Here—"

Tull had forgotten about him. "Stand away," he said. Trogdon backed up. Tull looked down into the weeping man's face. Tull stared at a spot on his temple, and imagined bringing the gun down upon it and cracking his skull like a pecan shell. But the man was no longer resisting him. Tull wiped some blood off the gun butt onto the man's pants, from which the stench of fresh shit was now rising. He stood up. Two Negroes who had been watching from across the street quickly turned and continued down the sidewalk. It was very nearly dark.

Trogdon was speechless, for once.

"Get your friend home," Tull said. "Thanks for your help."

He crossed Lombard toward Seventh Street without looking back, then disappeared around the corner. He had had it with Philadelphia.

10

They tell you Freedom is coming. They say Cross the river to Canaan's land. By which they mean Somewhere Else. Mr. Still said, "The Bondsman is not running *away* from slavery, but running *toward* freedom." Poor fool is always running *somewhere*. Where is it? What's he going to do when he gets there?

If I had a needle and thread,
Fine as I could sew,
I'd sew my good gal to my side,
And down the road I'd go.

And go where? Free to do what? Nobody asks that question. When you get there, will you have to go somewhere else?

They say the plantation is Paradise for master and Hell for the slave. But if you read Scripture, nothing happens in either place. Nothing changes; it's always *now*. I would have bit the apple, too. But if you get free, then you have to start running. As soon as *then* and *later* come in, it's time to go.

White people make up stories in their head about you and then they put you in the story and make you stay there. But as soon as you're in their story, you might as well be dead. If it doesn't have an end, it isn't a story. Never was a book yet ended on the word "and." If I ever wrote a book, that's how it would end. Maybe that would be the only word in the book. *And.*

The bird in a cage, he sings a song,
But the bird who's free flies all day long.

Where does he fly? And why?

If somebody opens the door to a cage and says, "Get in; I'll feed you," it's still a cage. Where's freedom? If you choose to be in a cage is that freedom? Why would you let somebody be your master? She volunteered to be a slave. Somebody ought to write a book about that.

Everybody wants to go to heaven, but nobody wants to die. Some people die to be free, but some people rather die than *be* free. Go away someplace with your freedom. They say, Free to do what? I'm happy here. Maybe they are right. As long as you're alive there's a chance of figuring it out, but I have a bad feeling maybe there's nothing to figure out. I have a bad feeling it's just questions all the way down.

But you won't see me crying. They won't catch me. I'll go straight up in the air like the Travelin' Man. Make a pair of shoes like Lost John:

Heels in the front, and heels behind,
Now nobody knows where Lost John gwine.

Here's a riddle:

My old mistress had a hen,
Black as any crow.
Laid three eggs every day,
Sunday she laid four.

That's all you get, and now I'm gone.

11

I managed to get through Thursday night's performance, barely. Mulligan took me aside afterward and asked if I were all right, and I told him I was. He looked at me from under his prodigious eyebrows, and I repeated that I was all right. But of course I was very disturbed, shaken by the appearance of the bounty hunter and the news he brought.

On Friday afternoon I arrived at the theater before the others, as usual. I had sent several messages to fellow minstrels who might be able to replace Henry, but I'd received no reply. I had no way of knowing if Henry would show up, nor of what the evening might bring. It was perhaps a quarter hour before six o'clock when I heard footsteps outside the dressing room. It was still early for any of the fellows to arrive, but when I went to the door I found myself face-to-face with Eagan, flushed, uncharacteristically minus cravat, and clearly upset about something.

"Michael," I said. "Are you all right?"

"Well," he said, "what are you going to do about this fellow now?"

"Which fellow?" I said.

"Come on, you know damn well who I'm talking about. You know damn well."

"I don't know," I said. "Damn well or otherwise."

"Your Colored protégé," he said. "Your black Don Juan."

"What do you mean, Eagan?" I said. "Consider before you say another word."

"I've had plenty of time to 'consider,' Douglass. He came to Rose's apartments last evening. Followed her home in secret, and asked her to come away with him."

"I don't believe that," I said. "Not for a minute."

"Don't you!" he said. "Turned up, begged her to let him stay with her overnight, and then when she denied him told her that she did not love me, and said she should come with him and sleep on the ground somewhere. In some nigger sty."

"Rose told you this?" I said.

"No, James—the man in the moon told me. What are you going to do about this? He said he was being hunted. He's a runaway, Douglass. Contraband. I'll turn him in myself if you do not."

"You'll do no such thing," I said. "I don't believe any of this. You'll keep a lid on yourself until I've spoken with both of them."

"The devil I will."

"You will," I said, "or you'll find another troupe to perform with."

"That won't be difficult, Douglass."

"Won't it?" I said, nearly beside myself. I was about to

cross a line into some untenable escalation with him, and one hour before curtain was no time for this. So I swallowed my anger and said, "Michael, please let us get on with the show, and we will sort things out afterward." Burke had arrived, and he caught my eye with a quizzical glance. I motioned him away.

"I will not appear onstage with that coon," Eagan said.

"You will not need to. Go prepare, and let me handle this."

So Henry knew he was being hunted. Perhaps he had already been caught. He might have left the city. Anything at all could have been true. Each scenario and its opposite seemed equally plausible. I had heard nothing back from Richards, nor from the two others to whom I had sent last-minute notes. So I sketched out a revised order for the second half, using the template of one of our weeknight shows, which did not feature Henry. I could not believe the story about showing up at Rose's. I was torn between pity for him and anger, at him and at myself. The damage he caused was mounting up.

Powell and Mulligan arrived in their turn. By half past six o'clock Henry had not shown up. I announced to the troupe that Henry was not going to appear, and I forestalled commentary by saying I would offer a full explanation afterward. I gave Eagan a significant look, which contained a command to keep his own counsel until I had straightened things out.

Mulligan took me by the arm. "James, I need to ask you something privately," he said, steering me out the dressing room door.

"What is going on, James?" he said when we were out of earshot. "You seem haunted. Is everything all right?"

I looked at him, then, my associate of years, and I saw genuine concern in his eyes. "Let's get through the evening, John," I said.

"Is Henry all right?"

I told him, quickly and in brief, what I knew, and what Eagan had said. His expression conveyed so much more of sorrow than any other emotion that I wondered if he had guessed the truth long before I had.

"The poor fellow," he said, when I had finished.

"There's nothing to be done now," I said.

The hour approached and we made our way to the stage, took our places. Gilman informed us that the house was nearly full. There would be disappointment, sharply expressed, when Demosthenes Jones failed to show, but we would carry on. We sat in our line, facing the curtain. At seven o'clock Gilman made his introductory announcement, and then I stomped my foot four times and the theater and its contents were once again severed from their moorings and we floated away.

The evening was warm, and the crowd spilled onto the sidewalk. He disliked crowds, and especially city crowds, and he waited outside until the performance was about to begin, savoring the last of the day's light as it drained from the sky and turned the buildings blue and gray. He wore a heavy jacket, inside of which he kept his pistol, a weighted folding knife, and a small wad of banknotes. The warm evening and slight breeze licked around the edges of his mood. All the Romes that rise and fall. The city one big stage set. The pure land that once was there. Across the darkening street was a tavern, and he let himself think that he might stop in afterward and uncouple himself from the week's preoccupations. But drink was poison to him, and he had lived with discipline for a long time. He liked it in the country, where people had their mind on fundamental things. Rain, crops, blood.

The inside of the theater was very busy, and Tull made his way to a seat through the pressing bodies, the tentative, groping others. Those who stood, absently, in place, taking up room and delaying his progress. He found a spot toward the back on the left, in a less-populated patch where he could have an unoccupied seat on either side. He did not enjoy the sustained proximity of other bodies, rowdy and unwashed. There was a small balcony overhead, but one never knew what one would find in the balcony. This theater was about the size of the Columbia in Richmond, which he had attended twice.

He removed his hat and kept it on the seat next to him to discourage company. It had been a long time since he had had a drink. There had been a period when he was a walking sponge, soaked and dripping whiskey all over the floor. He had wrung himself out, finally, hung himself in the sun to cure. The only time he ever felt the want of a drink was at times like these, in a city. The seats were filling. Someone standing in the center aisle was pointing to the seat next to him, inquiring if it was free. Tull waved him off.

He looked at the program. At the top of the second half were printed the words DEMOSTHENES JONES WILL APPEAR, with no further amplification. The curtains were closed. The house lights dimmed. A pair of men settled themselves in the seats immediately to Tull's left, and proceeded to bring out a flask.

A master of ceremonies strode out onto the stage and quieted the crowd, or tried to; he made an elaborate announcement, and then the curtain rose on the so-called Virginia Harmonists, five men seated in the standard minstrel line. Behind them, an elaborate painted backdrop of a plantation scene: two figures in knee breeches and long-tailed jackets, and three women in bright-colored hoop skirts, watching two smiling Darkies dance. A carriage with a smiling driver. Tull, unlike most of the people in the theater, was fully conscious of the distorted nature of the scene. The lie subscribed to by master and citizen alike, to preserve the myth of their own virtue. They hired the likes of him to do the rough work, behind the curtain. The frustrations of the week collected around this thought, and he reminded himself that he would be leaving the next day. He would try to enjoy the performance.

The fiddler was very good. The banjo player—they called him "Bullfrog Johnson," according to the program—was excellent. Tull was able to appreciate some of the finer points. He had seen minstrel shows in Richmond and, once, in Baltimore. He had learned some basic strokes on the banjo, which provided his sole purchase on beauty. There was a slave on the LaFontaine plantation near Appomattox, named Crito, who played both fiddle and banjo. He was a trustee, and came and went from LaFontaine more or less as he pleased. Every few weeks Crito would make the four-mile ride to Tull's cabin on a Sunday and they would sit on Tull's porch and play a few songs. Crito was a necessary figure for Tull, proof that the rest of his dark race was lazy and ignorant and dissolute by choice, not by the fact of their enslavement. They could be better if they wanted to.

The show went on. The two gallants on his left had prepared for their evening with a fair amount of whiskey, and they engaged in a dialogue about the presentation onstage, taking regular drinks from the flask and shouting at the performers.

"Dance, niggers!"

"Your trousers are too short!"

"Play that fiddle, Sam!"

Tull felt his irritation rising. Their remarks impinged upon his enjoyment of the presentation. Two useless characters who had probably never raised a callus from work.

"Have a drink?" The one next to him was offering him the flask. "Have a little fun why don't you?" Tull turned his head to regard him, unsmiling, and saw the fellow note his turned eye. The one nearest him wore a velvet tie and had a scar on his chin. Longish hair in back. The other had a full beard and wore a waistcoat and had his shirt buttoned to his neck. Tull stared at them without speaking.

The one next to Tull, still holding out the flask, returned Tull's stare and said, "Unfriendly. Did your husband turn you out for the night?"

Tull felt himself warming with a familiar pleasure. The speaker's companion on the other side saw Tull smile, and he tugged at his friend's arm and said, "Come on, let's move."

"Why?" said the one next to Tull. "He can move if he doesn't like our company."

With his left hand Tull grabbed the speaker's hair from behind, twisted the man's head, yanking it backward then

pushing it down quickly between the man's knees and leaning his weight on him. With his other hand Tull withdrew
the knife from his jacket pocket and with a flick of the wrist
opened it so that it locked into place.

"Here, what's this?" someone said in the row behind.

"Mind the show," Tull said to the voice. Tull looked across
his captive at the man's friend and raised his eyebrows.

"We'll go," the friend said. Onstage, the minstrels were
singing about some pretty dark-skinned girl they all loved.

Tull tightened his grip on his neighbor's hair and heard
him say, "We'll go."

"You're sure of that, right?" Tull said, leaning down.

"Yes," the voice said.

"All right." To the other, Tull said, "Go on out in the aisle.
Don't say anything."

The friend moved to the aisle, and Tull, keeping his grip
on his neighbor's hair, turned him and shoved him; the man
fell to the floor between the seats, recovered himself, and
joined his friend in the aisle. They departed.

Tull settled himself again in his seat, but the encounter had
put him in a foul humor. No one in the country would talk
that way. They would know they were inviting trouble. In the
city everything was a show. No consequences. He wondered
what the people around him would have thought if they visited a real plantation, with real slave quarters, real dirt and
blood. He would have liked to tie a few of them up and make
them watch a slave pissing himself with fear while Master
raped his wife in front of him. Let's see if they would dance a
jig to that. Let them smell the slop buckets outside the quarters and watch the little ones running around with no pants

on, shameless. Or take the Quakers, who thought all you had to do was wave your hand and say "You're free!" to turn one of these bucks into somebody who deserved to be free. All these faces turned toward the painted scenery on the stage. That's all they wanted to see. He got angrier as he sat there, with the crowd clapping and hollering around him.

The first half ended. Some of the audience lunged toward the lobby in search of pie or drink; the remainder stood at their seats, stretched, shouted to acquaintances across the hall. Tull had had enough. This show in this city where black criminals ran free, and these fools clapping along as if everything were fine. He would never track a runaway to a city again. He promised himself that.

He stood to leave and had started toward the aisle when his attention was caught by the sounds of a disturbance behind the stage curtain.

We got through the first half without discrediting ourselves and quit the stage for intermission. Our second half would be essentially the same as a typical weeknight program, although I shuffled some songs and switched a few for others so as not to repeat the previous night's list exactly. I was restless, and I paced backstage while the others sat and talked and refreshed their blacking in the dressing room.

One circuit took me behind our backdrop, toward stage right, where our unused stage scenery was stacked, and I noticed that the rear door, to the alley, was open. I had not opened it myself, and I went to investigate. I was about to shut and lock the door when I heard my name, hissed out from behind Birch's log cabin. I peered into the shadow. There, crouched behind the porch of the miniature Uncle Tom set, was Henry.

We regarded one another across a burning river.

"What are you doing?" I said.

"They found where I live," he said. "I can't go back. I need the banjo."

"We're at intermission."

"I'll leave," he said. "But I need the banjo."

"It's in the dressing room," I said. "What is this business with Rose? Did you go to her house?"

He did not respond.

"Are you out of your mind?" I said. He shook his head, and looked at me as if to ask, What do you want me to say?

I heard footsteps approaching. I turned and saw Mulligan, with an expression of shock on his blackened face.

"What's happened?" he said. "Why are you back here? Henry! Are you all right?"

"Hello, John," Henry said.

To me, Mulligan said, "What is going on?"

I was about to answer when I saw Eagan heading our way, yelling the words, "Black bastard!" Everything was suddenly going too quickly.

"Hold him off, John," I said.

Henry vaulted over a corner of the cabin porch, making for the stage, where the curtain was still down; Eagan dodged Mulligan and ran after Henry, getting a hand on his shirt at mid-stage. Henry wheeled around and struck Eagan in the face, and they crashed to the floor together, knocking over two chairs. Mulligan and I were on them almost immediately. Eagan yelled, "Nigger, I'll teach you a lesson!" We pulled him off Henry, who got to his feet and started for the dressing room again, but he tripped over a chair, and Eagan was out of our grasp and on him again. I noticed a rip under the arm of his jacket.

Powell and Burke and Gilman had appeared and were all in it now, but they were only adding to the confusion. I was trying to move the melee off stage. Ten paces from the dressing room, with Eagan subdued by the others, Henry got to his feet. God only knew what the audience was hearing, but this was a very bad situation. They had muscled Eagan to the other side of the stage and, with Mulligan's help, into the wings and out of our sight, and I had almost reached the dressing room door with Henry when a voice, at our heels, said, "Stop right there."

It was a beautiful scene, almost too perfect. He had known, intuitively, as soon as he heard the word ring out from behind the curtain, and now here it was. Climbed onto the stage, and had to knock someone out of the way to get behind the curtain. As if foretold, natural as a rainbow. There is an order of things, and it favored him. He gestured with the pistol.

"Nigger," Tull said, "you can bleed red just like a white man. Keep going." To the other he said, "I got him now." He followed the boy into the room, with the minstrel behind. Gesturing with the pistol toward a dressing-table chair, he kicked the door closed and said, "Sit down." The boy did. The green eyes, the light skin. The true fear in the eyes. Tull felt fountains of grace leaping around him, bright rubies and emeralds of truth. Even here, in this jungle, justice would find him. A white flame of purity shone upon him.

"Your daddy said dead or alive, Joseph," he said. "I don't care much one way or the other, but I think he misses you at dances. I got your banjo, too, that big nigger in the woodshop made."

Tull looked at the other man now, the minstrel, and under the blacking Tull recognized the person he had spoken to just the previous morning, in that same theater. He smiled and said, "I'm going to figure you didn't know, just like you said. I don't really care. Find some rope and help me get him tied."

The dressing room door opened and a large man entered, disarranged and with half the blacking gone from his face, followed quickly by another, shorter and animated. Tull recognized the short man as the fiddler. This one pushed past the larger man and started toward the captive.

"Ha!" he said. "Caught! I'll take a shot at him before you go . . ."

"Shut up," Tull said. He pointed his pistol at this short one, who halted immediately.

"What are you going to do with him?" said the first minstrel, the one from the day before.

"What do you care what I'm going to do with him?" Tull said. "What do you think I'm going to do with him? If you don't want this place shut down, get some rope and be quiet."

This first one hesitated, but the short fiddler said, "I'll help. I'll be glad to," and walked to an area behind a divan. Tull kept his eye on the man, who pushed away some pieces of stage detritus, props, a sign, a pair of Indian clubs. He hefted a coil of line and brought it to the stranger.

"You hold him," Tull said. To the large man he said, "You give me a hand tying."

"I will not," the big man said.

Tull focused on the big man, his energy darkening, then brightening in recognition. "Hey," he said. "You play a good banjo. Just stand over there by the door and be quiet while we get this done." To the boy, then, he said, "Remember, Joseph, your daddy said dead or alive. I'm happy either way." He removed his hat and set it on a chair.

The fiddler held the boy's legs as Tull tied them, quickly, his pistol within reach next to him on the floor. The others knew enough to stay put, at least, Tull thought. "I'm glad you all know the law," he said. "You almost had me, Joseph. I was getting ready to head out of town and tell your daddy you had slipped away. You're not as smart as they said."

When he was finished with the legs, Tull pushed the boy out of the chair and tripped him so that he was face-down on the floor, and the short minstrel knelt on the boy's shoulders. Tull looked around and said, "Get me some more rope."

"I can't breathe," the boy said. The fiddler had his wrists pinned behind his back.

"Ease up on him a little," Tull said.

The fiddler made some slight adjustment and said, to the boy, "They ought to hang you up and skin you. There, Douglass. What did I tell you? What did I say?"

"I don't want you talking," Tull said. "Where's the rope?" He bent over to perform some adjustments on the knots around the boy's legs.

"I'll get it," somebody said.

* * *

Eagan held Henry face-down in an arm lock, Mulligan stood by the door, and I stood to get another coil of rope. What else was there to do? And this, I thought, is how one forfeits one's soul. I could not bear to look at Henry. I would think that the image of such a scene would make God ashamed of his own creation, but I have become convinced, through many an ensuing year, that God has no shame.

What, after all, did I owe Henry? Did I force him at gunpoint to perform with us? Had I lied to him? Misrepresented the offer? Had he saved my life? Rescued me from a mob? I had not tricked him. I owed him nothing. I had built this troupe and thereby earned my freedom in this world of illusion, and I would not give it up. These men depended on the troupe as much as I did. We had bought ourselves time by presenting Henry, had regained our audience. With some diligence and luck we would keep their attention with other attractions. Henry would be taken away, captive, and we would remain free. I thought of how I had seen him perform on the street the first time. I thought of what it might have cost him to get himself free, to Philadelphia, the risks, the privation. Whom had he left behind? Where would he be taken? Was it my concern? My responsibility was to my men . . . I was in a fever. My partner, John, watched me as I stepped behind the divan to get the rope. I looked across the room at him, and our eyes met, and I hesitated for a moment. I saw him nod, very slightly. Eagan was taunting Henry.

I got hold of the required item and carried it across the room to where the stranger was bent over, tightening the ropes, and I swung that club as hard as I could into the base of the stranger's skull. I had kicked a rat once and felt the surprising weight of it against my toe, heard it expel something between a grunt and a squeal, and this figure made a similar sound as a mist of blood shot from his nose. Time slowed down, and I watched him fall forward at Henry's feet, like an orange onto a stack of towels, and roll to one side, unconscious. I watched as if from a tower, as if I were another, witnessing a riot in the square below. Then I went to strike him again, like a watermelon, turn his head to pulp. I would kill him. Mulligan was in front of me, blocking me. I recognized him, at least.

"Don't," he said. "James . . ."

I knew him; he was there. His hand was on my arm, and his eyes looked into mine as if from a distance.

"You'll go to jail for this!" Eagan was saying. "I'll see to it."

Mulligan said, "I will put an end to you if you say another word, Michael." He bent down and retrieved the pistol. "Sit and be quiet, or you'll be sorry."

The stranger was unconscious; a trickle of blood ran from his left nostril down his cheek and into his long, greasy hair. He was breathing. Henry had rolled onto his side, and Mulligan knelt to untie him. I was looking at Henry struggling to get free even faster. Then he was untied, and standing, and Mulligan was pulling some banknotes from his pocket, but before he could offer them, Henry was gone—out the door, disappeared, just that quickly, not a goodbye, just gone. Gone. I had not been able to utter a word to him.

Somewhere overhead the stars wheeled in the evening sky, unseen. I was shaking; I was so cold. I could not stop shaking. Mulligan stayed with me and very shortly two men identifying themselves as police officers arrived, no more than two minutes after I had struck the stranger. One of them, with sandy hair and long side whiskers, seemed to recognize the still-unconscious figure.

"You did this?" he said.

"Yes," I said.

He nodded, mulling it. His companion, a half-wit wearing an odd hat, said, "He gave poor Vic the beating. We spent the entire day for two dollars."

I was taken into custody, and put in the city jail for a week, until, through the efforts of a businessman I did not even know—a Negro, in the bargain, named Still—I was released, my crime deemed self-defense. Apparently he had had some dealings, himself, with Henry. I never found out what happened to the bounty hunter; all I was told was that he had not died, and had left the city.

But it was the end of the Virginia Harmonists.

Eagan, Powell, and Burke formed their own troupe. Mulligan left, for Boston, inviting me to come with him and establish a new troupe there. But I had lost my taste for minstrelsy. Not for the music, but for the overwhelming lie upon which it fed. Some fluid that had surrounded me had evaporated. The magic Henry had summoned had ended in such violence and discord, and I could not help but imagine all the others in similar straits, or worse. Seeing it had closed off an avenue which had been my road in life, and I was at a loss, as if I were suddenly unable to write, or walk.

I took a job for a while as stage manager at Sanford's, but the presence of all that enforced gaiety onstage in contrast with the reality behind it, and the sheer tedium involved in my job, chafed intolerably. Things began to seem pointless, as pointless as they had seemed at the farm. I struggled to remain at the theater, but I felt that if I did so I would cede the final measure of any dream I had sustained through the years, destroy my past as well as whatever the future might bring, and at length I quit. And then, for a time, I drifted.

Not quite a year later, I was walking along Front Street. I had fallen on difficult times, had moved from my apartments off Washington Square into more affordable quarters, and I often spent the afternoons walking aimlessly through the Philadelphia streets, hoping, I suppose, that I might once again stumble upon some unexpected grace, some magic that could assure me that everything I saw was more than a veneer with nothing behind it, that a caring God still existed.

I had just passed Shippen Street, heading south into a rough quarter, when I saw an unmistakable figure walking half a block away, in front of me. I could not believe my own eyes, and I quickened my pace to catch up, and when I was several paces behind, and sure of who I saw, I called out, "Rose!"

The figure spun around to face me. I saw that she recognized me quickly enough, although I had certainly put on flesh. She had, as well; clearly, she was with child.

"Rose!" I said, again.

"Hello, James," she said, flatly.

What a mixture of emotions coursed over me then. Her hair was still short, yet not carefully attended to. She wore a skirt that went only to her calves, and a shapeless blouse. The skin on her face was drawn, and I noticed a reddish, dry patch on her elegant neck. She was still lovely, yet her features wore an expression from which the light had all but disappeared. A crease had formed between her eyebrows.

"How are you?" I asked, putting out my hand, hoping for a touch of hers on mine.

"I'm well, James," she said, with no expression, taking my hand briefly and then letting hers fall back to her side.

"Do you live here?" I asked. "In this neighborhood, I mean?"

"I stay nearby," she said. She looked up and down the block.

"Please," I said, "do you have time for a visit? We can go to Tanner's."

"No," she said, "I should not." She did not seem absolutely sure of this, and I asked again if we might at least sit and visit outside for a while, and she relented.

I bought two buns for us at a bakery a block away, and we took them and sat on some piled-up rocks that served as a partial levee between docks on the river's edge. It was a beautiful early spring afternoon, and we unwrapped the waxed paper around our bread and ate, talking and looking out at the Delaware. I told her of how the year had gone; she had heard about the melee, of course. I told her that I was retired from performing, that it had lost its appeal, and she seemed saddened by this, but not surprised. I did not mention that I had moved down somewhat in the world, although I am sure that was clear enough on the face of things. She asked about Mulligan, and I told her he had gone to Boston. She did not ask about Henry.

I had lost track of her after the troupe disbanded, assumed

she had gone with Eagan and the others, and I told her this, asked how the fellows were. She told me she had not seen Eagan for the better part of a year.

"But why?" I said. "I had thought you would follow them to their new theater . . . ?"

"I did," she said. "But Michael tired of me."

"Tired of you?" I said. "That is impossible!" I believe that I meant this to sound lighthearted, and I saw her attempt to summon a smile in return, but her features expressed only a sadness that nearly broke my heart.

"He accused me of being unfaithful," she said. "I don't know if he even believed that himself. I think he just wanted to be rid of me."

"Well . . ." I said, hesitant to ask a further question. "I can't understand that."

"Can't you?" she said.

"Are you with another troupe now?"

She shook her head in the negative. "I do piecework. I make my living as I can. As you can see, I will have a dependent soon."

"Is it . . . Eagan's child?" I blurted out.

"No, James," she said. "It is not Eagan's child."

We sat silently for a while longer, as I struggled to think of what to say. At length, Rose said, "I ought to go."

"Rose," I said. We stood up, and I felt something rushing through my hands that I would never again touch, and I felt a kind of panic rise in me, and on impulse I said, "Come to live with me. I'm not in the finest place, but I will take care of you as well as I can. Please—we can still make something of our lives, together."

Even as I was saying these words I watched her expression darken into a frown, a wounded look, and she stepped back from me.

"What's wrong?" I said.

"Oh," she said. "You are still a child." She drew her arms around herself, looked as if she might say something else, then she turned and walked, quickly, away. And I stood there, dumbly, watching her.

That encounter broke something final inside me, as if a cyst had burst and the last store of boyish hope, and fear—the best in me, perhaps, and perhaps also the worst—began to dissipate. If I had not, until then, finished with being a boy, now I surrendered my papers. I pulled myself together and got a job working in, then managing, a lumber warehouse. I gradually returned to a more stable financial footing, recovered an aptitude for lists and receipts. I counted and stacked and counted again.

Yet as I left that island of boyish illusion behind, I found myself wondering more and more often what had happened to Henry. Had he managed to find a place where he could settle? Had he managed to stay free? I had never wholly known him, and yet he had meant something much more to me even than I had realized at the time, more as the months and years went by. The freedom he had claimed for himself, in spite of enslavement. I wondered if he had found a place of safety. I never would have an answer to that question.

Then, one evening, borne on some rogue breeze, I found myself in front of the New Walnut Theater, with its placard outside, a stream of people lining up for tickets and entering, and I decided to join the crowd, enter and see the show. It was a new troupe, one that made a specialty of "original Darky minstrelsy." Enough time had gone by that the original five-man troupes were again something of a novelty, though they drew an audience half the size ours had been at Barton's. The names on the showbill were unfamiliar to me.

I went in, took my seat, and waited, as if in two places at once—in front of, and also behind, the proscenium. I could imagine them getting ready in the dressing room, imagine them settling in the chairs behind the curtain, making final adjustments. At length, the master of ceremonies appeared and made his announcement, and then the curtain rose to the tambourine's *whack* and a voice declaiming, "*Good ebening, everybody!*" The audience leapt up around me, shouting and clapping, and I remained seated and heard the line sail into "Lucy Long," and the song did make me smile, and when the audience had gotten seated again, and clapped along, I watched in bittersweet pleasure. I still loved the beautiful illusion, even as I saw through it. How could I not? If someone were to promise that it was possible to dance in the teeth of oppression and affliction, to cast away the frailty of age, the attrition of illness, the weight of every mistake one had made in life, possible to be absolved from every wrong you had done and witness your accusers singing your praises . . . Well, pilgrims would arrive from every point on the globe to be told this, though they knew it to be a lie. The show went on, and the show went on, and I was there, and I was not there. I knew too much about it all, and the illusion was gone from me. Yet still I rejoiced, and still I wept.

PART
IV

12

There is nothing better than a macaroon. Unless it is a cherry tart from Leininger's. If I spill a crumb or two, Addie keeps at me until I clean it up myself. At those times I offer protest by calling her by her given name, Frances, and she pretends not to notice. Or perhaps she does not, in fact, notice. I remind her that I am a senator, that my time is in demand, that I will soon leave Auburn again and travel back to Washington and she will miss me, and in reply she hands me a list of items that need attending around the property, a few names of our latest petitioners, pet social causes to which she would like me to lend my support.

"Thank you, sweetheart," I say.

"I thought my name was Frances," she says, walking away.

Who can explain love? All our children are gone, now, except for darling Fanny. If I had any illusions about spending more time alone with Addie, they have been subverted by the very energies that drew me to her in the beginning.

She is on fire with the abolitionist fever, with which I am in complete sympathy, although other considerations demand a degree of moderation and perspective from myself, as I look toward a time in which I may be called to be President of the entire republic. Still, her single-mindedness in aiding fugitives, and even, upon occasion, hiding them for a brief spell in our basement, is to be admired and supported, and I do.

At any rate we have little enough time together, so I must have expressed some inadvertent displeasure, or at least reservation, when she informed me that there would be another "guest" taking up residence below our house for some unspecified amount of time.

"Ah," I said. "Good."

"You needn't bristle, Bill. I doubt that he will be here long."

"Of course," I said.

"Is there any reason of which I'm unaware that we shouldn't offer shelter to him?"

"Not at all."

"There was a time when you would have expressed no reservations at all about aiding anyone who had suffered under the lash."

"I am in complete agreement that we should help this one as well," I said.

She regarded me severely for a long moment. "You would drive a sensible person to morphine." She turned and started away.

"When will he arrive, dear?" I offered.

"Tomorrow," she said, shutting my office door with no excess of decorum.

The fact is that I was in complete agreement, here. I merely had . . . reservations. Yet when I would bring up my desire to spend more time alone with her, Addie would say, "Then why do you always run to Washington? Or Albany? Or Philadelphia?"

"My work takes me there," I say.

"Then don't begrudge me mine."

She would have made a good attorney, God save us all.

I was always bedeviled by strange fancies. You can't know what it is to present yourself constantly to the world as a figurehead of state, while inside you have as much imagination as any man. More! So while I greeted visitors, made speeches, drafted resolutions, plotted strategy, I also had visions of unexplainable things—sometimes they were merely whimsical: talking spiders, goats dancing. Colors often looked odd to me, as if they had distinct personalities. I thought of fires blanketing the horizon, bodies of the dead walking through smoke on a field. Songs played on strangely shaped instruments. There was a time, about which no one knows except Addie, when I had to take to bed for a week, overcome as I was with it all. These visions did not disappear, exactly, but rather I would say they retreated into place; I learned how to cohabit with them, and when they saw that I would make room for them they became less urgent, less threatening and shrill.

Often I would seek out one or another of our servants at such times. I found that a visit while they were doing a job they understood had a calming effect on me, as if it represented an unarguable degree of reality. I had always enjoyed visiting with my father's kitchen help, and I enjoyed visiting with Ella when she prepared dinner. Nicholas and I never seemed quite to engender a rapport—he was a church man—but I enjoyed hearing Ella's thoughts on politics and town gossip.

It was and is my firm conviction that the degree of civilization in a culture—practical, ethical, spiritual—is measured not by the grandeur of its edifices nor the extent of its land holdings but by the way in which those who hold and administer power treat those over whom they may exercise that power, whether it is a jailer with a captive, a parent with a child, or a lender with a debtor. If one has the upper hand in a situation, and uses it to exploit another to that other's detriment, one cannot call oneself civilized. By that measure, perhaps, none of us can call himself fully civilized. Yet one may strive for that ideal, at least. Otherwise one's career as a decent human being is at an end.

The young man was delivered to us just after nightfall, during dinner, on a very cold evening toward the end of November. For obvious reasons, I cannot reveal the name of the Friend who had arranged for this and delivered him, but this Friend had indicated that the young man was quite unusual and articulate, had just run off from a Maryland plantation, and was reticent about going to Canada but had accepted aid in that direction after some convincing. He would put up in the basement room that we had fitted out for that purpose. I would imagine that we had harbored some two dozen fugitives there over the space of three or four years.

Before dinner, I asked Addie if our Friend had confirmed the passenger's arrival that evening.

"Yes," Addie replied. "He has a banjar and not much else."

"A banjar!" I said. "We will have music, then."

"Take this out back," she said, handing me a slop bucket.

I loved the smell of woodsmoke in the biting cold. That sense of winter coming on, the quickening attention—I missed it all in Washington, with its moderate Southern climate. I disposed of the slops in their appointed place. On my way back to the house I saw a bright-red maple leaf on the walkway, almost perfect—remarkable, as the autumn colors had quite retired for the year—and I brought it inside as a late addition for Fanny's leaf collection, which she kept in a large scrapbook I had purchased for her.

That evening, as we were having dessert, we heard a knocking at our rear door in a deliberate and familiar pattern. Addie glanced across the table at me and then excused herself.

"Well, Fanny," I said. "We will have a new guest for a day or two. What do you think of that?"

"It makes me sad," she said.

"Why ever does it make you sad, Fanny?"

"They have no home."

My darling was not just sensitive but she was intelligent, and she had instincts for what was morally correct. I love her so. I did not know how to address this concern of hers. I also knew that my protracted absences weighed on her, as they did on Addie.

"Did you place the leaf in your album?"

She nodded. Ella brought in more coffee.

"All is going well?" I asked.

"They're getting him settled," she replied.

"You'll bring supper to him?"

"Once they get him settled I will."

"Why can't he eat with us?" Fanny said.

"Darling," I said, "he will be tired from his travels." But the runaways never ate with us, even when they stayed for two or three days. This was Addie's policy—something of an inconsistency, I thought, as she was such an ardent abolitionist. Yet I had learned over the years to let her manage her end of things without questioning.

At length, Addie reappeared and settled herself at her end of the dinner table, and Ella brought her some fresh coffee.

"All is well?" I said.

She nodded thoughtfully, and took a long sip of the hot coffee.

"What is wrong?" I said.

"Nothing is wrong," she said. "You might go down and greet him yourself."

"Yes, of course," I said. "I was waiting for you to finish getting him situated."

"He is situated," she said. "There is something unusual about him."

"What do you mean?"

"You'll see for yourself," she said. "I can't put my finger on it."

"What is his name?"

"He is called William."

"Well," I said. "Perhaps I'll go downstairs and welcome him."

"Yes, that would be a good idea," she said. "Fanny, didn't you like your tart?"

I excused myself and quit the dining room and nearly ran into Ella coming up from the basement. She looked as if she had just had a good laugh.

"Is everything all right?" I asked.

"Yes, sir, just fine."

I found him downstairs, in the room we used for our "passengers," as they were sometimes called—it was in fact our old kitchen. He stood up as soon as he saw me. One could tell immediately that there was something different about him, as Addie had indicated. A kind of quickness about the eyes, perhaps—green eyes, with something almost feminine about them. Most of these guests had a deferential air and were not quick to meet one's eyes. This William was not afraid to meet one's gaze with a gaze of his own. I do not mean to say that it gave offense, only that one was unaccustomed to meeting such an expression in a Negro. He was rather short of stature, and he wore a plaid flannel shirt buttoned to his neck, braces, and a straw hat which he remembered to remove only after several seconds had passed.

"Welcome," I said. "I see you have supper; I won't keep you. Your travels were satisfactory?"

"Yes," he said. "Where am I?"

I could not suppress a brief chuckle at the ingenuousness of the question. "You are in Auburn, New York. Our friend didn't tell you where you were going?"

"He told me we were in Auburn, but I didn't know where it was. Are we close to Canada?"

"Fairly close," I said. "You are anxious to get there, of course."

"No," he said. "I don't want to go to Canada."

I could see now what Addie meant. The usual air of submission was absent.

"Well, then, where are you hoping to go?" I said.

"I don't know," he said. We stood regarding one another for a few moments, and then he said, "They said you're a senator."

"Yes," I said. "They said you play the banjar."

He laughed at this—at the nature of the exchange, it seemed, rather than the substance. "I do."

"Well, I hope that before you leave here you will play some music for us."

His eyes widened in surprise.

"Or not," I said. "If you do not wish to."

"No," he said, "I will."

"Good, then," I said. "Well. Please don't let your supper get cold. And I should rejoin my family. Perhaps after dinner, a bit later? If you are so inclined."

He nodded; the expression on his face was odd indeed, a simultaneous frown and smile. I took my leave and went back upstairs.

"I see what you mean about our guest," I said. "I asked him to play on the banjar for us after dinner."

"The boy has just arrived, Bill. Let him catch his breath."

I saw that Fanny had instantly brightened at the idea, though, and her pleasure was ours, always.

After the table was cleared and we had had our coffee, I went downstairs and found our guest sitting in the small rocking chair, looking at loose ends, an expression of sadness on his face. Across the narrow mattress at the far end of the room was a banjar. I had the odd sensation that there were two people in the room, the fellow and the instrument.

"You know," I said, "we are both named William."

"What?" he said. He seemed slightly confused by this information. "Should I call you William?"

I was taken aback at this, and quickly reminded myself that the majority of slaves had not had extensive instruction in etiquette, and to be patient. "Why don't you call me Senator," I said, trying to be reassuring. "You may call Mrs. Seward 'Mrs. Seward,' and our daughter Fanny is Miss Seward."

"I'm sorry!" he said.

"No, no. Nothing to be sorry for. Will you come and play for us?"

He stood, crossed the room, and picked up his instrument. I had a pang, then, watching him, as I had so many, trying to comprehend the degree of dislocation, the sheer strangeness of being in a strange house, among strangers, no matter how well-intentioned, in a strange town set into a strange countryside. I thought that Addie might have been right, and that I was forcing the boy to do something he was not ready to do. But I love music so, and Fanny does, as well.

"You do not need to play for us," I said. "This evening, or ever. I hope I am not . . ."

"No," he said, "I'm happy to play. Some don't like it."

"Well," I said, "anyone who does not welcome music into his home has some terminal deficiency of spirit."

He smiled, nodded, and we walked up the stairs.

Addie and Fanny had taken their places in our parlor. I saw William looking around as we walked through the dining room; our house is well stocked with paintings and various artifacts that I have managed to gather on my travels across the country and around the world, and the young man took it in as if he were a pilgrim at the Sistine Chapel. I thought that I would give him a more detailed tour if he showed interest, perhaps the next morning.

"Don't put him on that little stool, Bill," Addie said.

"But his arms will need room if he's to play the banjar," I offered.

Addressing the young man, she said, "Come here and sit in this good chair."

"You have met my wife, Mrs. Seward."

"We've already met, Bill," Addie said, installing him in an armchair where she often crocheted of an evening.

"And this," I said, "is my daughter Fanny."

I saw the young man regard her with a look of tenderness and even mutual understanding. "Hello, Miss Seward," he said.

Fanny beamed and said, "My name is Fanny!"

William looked at me, and with a shrug I tried to indicate that my world was ruled by women, and that he should submit to the same law.

He sat in the proffered chair.

"Would you like anything to refresh yourself, William?" Addie said to our guest.

"No, thank you," he said.

We all arranged ourselves—Addie and Fanny on our divan, and myself in my own chair. Nicholas had gotten a good fire underway. The young man set to tuning his banjar with an extraordinary concentration, and we all three watched him until he had got the strings pitched to his satisfaction.

"Is there anything you would like to hear?" He addressed this to the room, but his gaze alighted on Fanny, and his eyebrows went up and she blushed.

"Can you play 'Angelina Baker'?" she asked.

I saw Addie's face tighten a bit, and then she said, "Fanny, perhaps another song," and she sent me a stern look. I happened to be quite fond of the song, but Addie disliked it because of its plantation theme. Of course I sympathized, and played it, badly, on the pianoforte only when she was not around. It was a favorite of Fanny's, and I think Addie blamed me for instilling a fondness for the "Darky" songs in our daughter.

William looked across the room at me, and I spoke up. "At your pleasure, William."

He smiled at Fanny, and said, "That's one of my favorites, too." To Addie, he said, "May I play it for her?"

Impossible to say no under the circumstances. Addie managed a smile and said, "Go ahead."

He began the familiar tune simply, on his banjar, and after his initial tour of the melody started singing:

Way down on de old plantation,
Dat's where I was born.
I used to beat de whole creation
Hoein' in the corn . . .

I will admit that it was an odd sensation, listening to those lyrics we had sung with such gusto, coming from the mouth of one who had suffered under the lash. Addie was visibly uncomfortable. Still, Fanny and I joined in happily on the refrain,

Angelina Baker! Angelina Baker's gone;
She left me here to weep a tear
And beat on the old jaw bone . . .

He sang the song but one time through, then played it twice on the banjar with wonderful variations, and even Addie allowed herself an exclamation of surprise and appreciation when he had finished. I was touched to see Fanny and the young man exchange a complicitous glance and smile at one another. The fellow carried himself like a young knight of olden times, I thought.

"Ma'am," he said, addressing Addie, "do you have a special favorite?"

"Do you sing 'Go Down, Moses'? Or 'Thorny Desert'?"

These two songs were abolitionist standards. Both were favorites of our friend, the well-known Tubman. I thought I saw William disguise a wince, or perhaps it was my own wince that I saw reflected in his face. At any rate, he sang the spiritual 'Go Down, Moses' *a capella*, once through, and Addie sat with her eyes closed, swaying slightly to the song's cadences. When he had finished, she said, "That was quite beautiful. Thank you."

This fellow, I was certain, had had experience on the stage, or at least performing somewhere for audiences, for he had us entirely under his spell.

He asked what my request might be, and I said, "Play one of your own favorites. Something that pleases you."

"Well," he said, thoughtfully, adjusting one of his tuning pegs until it obeyed some law that only he perceived. A familiar melody materialized under his fingers now, with its irresistible rhythm, and he started singing.

Old Dan Tucker was a fine old man,
Washed his face in a frying pan.
Combed his hair with a wagon wheel,
Died with a toothache in his heel . . .

We all joined in for the rousing chorus:

Get out the way, Old Dan Tucker.
You're too late to get your supper!

What fun it was. At length, Addie broke the spell by saying, "Young man, you must be tired from traveling, and I am afraid that we are imposing on your good nature by making you entertain us. Your bed is ready, below, and you should feel free to retire at any time."

"Thank you, Mrs. Seward," he said, "but you are not imposing. I hope I'm not imposing. This is fun."

Addie appeared a bit taken aback by his response, although it seemed an entirely credible statement to me; he seemed to come alive while he was playing and singing. He did retire, though, and we did as well.

As we went upstairs, darling Fanny said, "I am so glad William is here with us!"

"Did you enjoy that, sweetheart?"

She nodded vigorously, and I kissed her, and Addie took her to her bedroom. As I prepared for the night I thought about how remarkable it was that a fellow in his situation could summon such gaiety and poise, and share it with others whom he scarcely knew.

* * *

The next morning after breakfast I opened the basement door and went down to check on our "passenger." He was sitting at a small table, finishing the meal Ella had prepared for him. This would be a day of finding him clothes and getting him ready for the next part of his journey. He stood up when I appeared, but I insisted that he sit back down, and I took a seat on the narrow bed, which I noticed he had made.

"Did you sleep well?" I asked.

"I did," he replied. "Thank you. I like this room."

"You do," I said. "What do you like about it?"

"It brings back pleasant memories."

The notion that a slave might have any pleasant memories was surprising to me. I would have thought that a runaway would be glad to erase any memories of his servitude, and I said something to that effect.

His face registered that peculiar smile-frown I had noted the night before. He merely nodded and said nothing.

I had business, involving a visit to associates in Seneca Falls, which would consume most of the day into the afternoon, and I bade our guest relax and enjoy himself. The idea was that the lad would remain with us for two full days and three nights, renewing himself before being "conducted" on the final part of his journey to freedom. As I was about to take my leave he begged my pardon and asked if it were possible to borrow a book, for the day.

He was, indeed, full of surprises. "A book!" I said.

To save me the embarrassment, I suppose, of asking an impolite question or showing any more surprise, he said, "My mother taught me to read."

"Certainly," I said. "Certainly. Come with me."

Addie had gone to market and Fanny was at lessons. Ella was somewhere about, as was Nicholas, and I saw no harm in leading the fellow upstairs to my library. In truth, the entire house was in the process of becoming a library, as Addie often complained, but I thought William might enjoy seeing my own sanctuary on the second floor, as it had some interesting prints and artifacts from my travels, along with a wall of books, among which I was certain he might find something worth perusing.

As we entered the room his face registered a gratifying degree of surprise and appreciation. After a moment or two he asked me how I located a book, among so many.

"They are arranged by subject," I said, "and then by author, within each subject. History is here," I indicated the area with my hand. "Here are philosophy, books on travel, botany . . ." I wondered what he thought, seeing it all there. Did it represent a window onto possibility, a vista of worlds to be attained, or did it represent instead an unscalable wall intended exactly to keep him out? I had my answer almost immediately.

"Do you have any by Dickens?" he said.

"Of course," I replied. Absolutely extraordinary, I thought. I lent him the first volume of *Pickwick*, and *American Notes*, pointing out that the author had had interesting things to say about our peculiar institution of slavery. "This ought to keep you busy until we see one another this evening."

I got him settled again in our subterranean room and went on about my business for the day, yet I could not get him out of my mind. I found myself, to my surprise, wishing that his stay with us might be extended. It occurred to me that there might be a mutual profit in bringing him to Rochester and introducing him to Frederick Douglass, surely a visit that would be of interest to them both.

Late that afternoon I arrived home, and there was a fine fire going, preparations for dinner in progress. Addie was going through some papers at the escritoire, and I stooped to kiss her cheek.

"Is everything all right, dear?" I asked.

"Everything is fine. Did you initiate a subscription to a newspaper? Or cancel a subscription?"

"Not that I can think of," I replied. "We take the *Standard* and the *Times*, I believe? Why do you ask?"

She frowned, shrugged. "It is nothing. Someone came to the door this afternoon and spoke to Ella about newspapers, and she did not have a clear idea of what the man was saying."

"What did he want?"

"I don't know, Bill. He said something about newspapers. He probably had the wrong address."

"We really ought to make it an inflexible rule that Nicholas answer the door and not Ella," I said.

"Well, Bill, Nicholas was occupied, and Ella does the best she can . . ."

"Yes, of course; please let's not quarrel. I will speak with her."

"I already have. Never mind."

Fanny, I knew, would be upstairs at her lessons, and I thought I would stop downstairs and see how our guest had spent the day.

He was reading when I descended, and he put the book down and stood up. "How are you enjoying Dickens?" I asked. "Please sit down." We took the same places we had taken that morning.

"Have you been to England?" he said.

"I have not," I replied. "Why do you ask?" And then, "Oh. Of course."

"He doesn't like America much," he said.

"I think their attitude toward us is mixed," I said. "Perhaps we exercise a freedom that they wish for, and yet which their sense of manner, or propriety, tells them is somehow vulgar."

His face registered a degree of amusement at this remark, and I asked him what he had found amusing.

"Dickens always sympathizes with people having a hard time," he replied.

"Yes," I said. "That he does." What a fellow, I thought. "Listen, would you enjoy it if we had cigars later, after dinner? Have you ever had a cigar? I could bring down a pair and we could have a proper visit."

He seemed faintly stunned by the idea, but he said if that was what I wanted to do he would be pleased to join me.

"Wonderful!" I said. "I'll bring some brandy as well."

At dinner, Fanny asked several times whether William would join us again and play the banjar.

"Dear," Addie said, "the young man is not here for our entertainment. I imagine that he has been ordered about quite enough in his short life."

Fanny's feelings were hurt by the remark, and I said to Addie, "Perhaps the fellow can come and sit with us again for a short visit tonight? He is here so briefly."

When we had finished coffee I invited William upstairs. We all assumed our positions from the previous evening, and there was some stilted talk. I had the sense that the fellow would have felt more comfortable playing music for us. After a few minutes of this, William regarded Fanny and said, "Do you know how to make a fireplace match disappear?"

"Throw it out the window!" she said.

"That's the best way." he said. "But what if there is no window?" She appeared to think hard, and after some moments, the fellow said, "Would you like me to show you the best way?"

"Yes!"

"May I take a fireplace match?" he said, addressing Addie.

"They are right there," Addie said, indicating a shelf to the side of the mantel.

William plucked one of the thin wooden sticks and broke off a stem about two inches in length, displayed it so that Fanny could see it, also meeting my eyes, and Addie's, with an expression of great seriousness. He situated the match between index finger and thumb, made sure we saw it, and then with a plosive gesture opened his hand and the match was gone. As we fairly gaped, William's face expressed a degree of discomfort, then pain, and he reached to his ear and pulled, as if a thorn were lodged there, and retrieved the troublesome length of matchstick, displaying it for us once again.

We all applauded. Fanny was in transports of delight, and begged him to repeat the trick, and he did so, this time leaving his chair and retrieving the match from behind Fanny's ear.

"How do you make it disappear?" she pleaded.

With mock solemnity, he replied that it took long training and great discipline.

At length it was time for Fanny to go to bed, and Addie said she would retire as well. I said that I would be up in a while. William went downstairs, and a quarter hour later I descended the steps into the basement, managing to carry a decanter of brandy and two glasses, with two good cigars in my breast pocket. I opened one of the casement windows, located near the low ceiling and giving out onto the ground level, so that the cigar smoke would not seep upstairs and disturb Addie.

"Do you drink brandy at all?" I asked, arranging things a bit and lighting another candle.

"No," he said.

"Well," I said. "Will you have one with me?" I set the glasses out on a little table and poured myself a modest draw, and another for him. "Here's to your good fortune in the future, William."

"Thank you," he said. We took our first sips of the fine, fiery brandy, which blazed a warm trail down the inside of my chest and into my stomach. He examined the liquid through the glass, against the candlelight. I remarked to myself how difficult, perhaps impossible, it was to see into the mind, or through the eyes, of one who had been born a slave. So many things that we take for granted must be nearly miracles to them.

"Here," I said, producing the cigars. "These are made in Havana. Do you know where that is?"

"Cuba! That's where Spanish Pete was from."

"Spanish Pete," I said. "Tell me who he was."

"He used to sort the crops for market. Or he'd divide them into house vegetables, market vegetables." He held the cigar to his nose. "That smells good," he said.

I was mulling what he'd said, since so many bondsmen were from the West Indies and spoke French, or variants thereof, rather than Spanish.

"Do you know how Pete happened to come to where you lived? It was a farm, of course?"

He nodded and said, "In Virginia. I don't know how he got there. He was just there. He taught me how to speak Spanish."

"You can speak Spanish!" I said. "Say something to me in Spanish!"

"*Mariposa la basura de quanto varieades de supuesto!*"

"That is not Spanish!" I said. But he was laughing at the expression on my face. His accent, be it said, was perfect, although the words were utter nonsense. I found myself laughing along with him. "I hope you didn't pay him for lessons!"

"No," he said. "It was all out in the barn."

I refilled our glasses and gestured to him to direct the smoke toward the window I had opened. "Addie—Mrs. Seward—does not encourage me to smoke in the house."

We smoked our cigars and drank our brandy and talked easily, without a fixed direction or agenda, and I won't be overstating if I say that it was one of the most enjoyable hours I had spent in recent memory. He spoke of seeing and hearing traveling musicians when he was a boy—he was yet little more than a boy, for that—and of being shown the secrets of the banjar by an older man who worked in the wood shop at the farm. He spoke of playing for dances at the farm, and of the river that ran alongside the property, the boats that came and went. The smell of food cooking, and the tasks at the wood shop. When he spoke of the farm, an odd quality of melancholy, or nostalgia, seemed to reveal itself. He spoke of the afternoon sun as it came in through the wood shop door and illuminated the wood shavings on the floor. He spoke of the fellow, Enoch, who came back from being hired out in the city, wearing a red silk scarf, and the wonder this engendered in him, and of hearing the banjar for the first time. The world was a simple one as he rendered it—a place with a wood shop, a dairy, a mansion house. I had the oddest feeling that he, or some part of him, yearned for that relative simplicity, and I asked him about that. "You sound almost as if you miss the place," is what I said.

He reacted as if I had suggested the most preposterous idea imaginable. "Miss it!" he said. "I would not go back there for anything." But on his face was the saddest expression I think I have ever seen. We went on to other things, but my mind stayed with that paradox which had presented itself. How would one manage to live in the world, carrying that peculiar burden of nostalgia for an intolerable situation? What were the costs of leaving a place whose familiarity both sustained you and threatened to extinguish you?

He told me he had performed onstage, with a minstrel troupe for which he needed to black his own face, although he was evasive on the topic of where this was. I asked him if he had ever tried to compose a song of his own.

He demurred at first, but at length he agreed to deliver it for me.

"Just not at full voice," I said. "Let's not bring Addie's wrath down upon us."

He set his glass down rather deliberately—I sensed that he was feeling the brandy's effects—and, cigar clenched in his teeth, reached to the bed and picked up his banjar and set it in his lap, strummed down softly and did his usual string adjustments as I poured myself another small shot of the brandy. I gestured an offer to him but he declined.

The banjar in tune, he began a jaunty rhythm on the strings and in short order commenced singing. I later wrote down the words as well as I could remember them:

Hoe cakes in the mornin'
Chicken at dinnertime
Whiskey when I'm thirsty
Heaven when I'm dyin'.
It's a fine old world for some folks
And I take it as I can
Today I'm just a Darky
Someday I'll be a man.

I went down South to see my gal
I did not go to stay
Patateroller caught me
And I could not get away.
It's a fine old world for some folks
And I take it as I can
Today I'm just a poor old slave
Someday I'll be a man.

They beat me and they cursed me
They tore off all my clothes

They put me in that cotton field
And called me Little Mose
They had a man to watch us
He sat astride a horse
I never did find out his name
We had to call him "Boss."
It's a fine old world for some folks
And I take it as I can
Today they call me nigger
Someday I'll be a man.

At night I dream of Freedom
By day I dream the same
Someday I'll go to Canaan's land
And have a brand-new name.
It's a fine old world for some folks
And I take it as I can
I'll head up North where folks are free
And stand up like a man.

When he had finished, he avoided my eyes, made a few adjustments to the strings, reached for his cigar on the table, as I sat, groping for words. I was quite undone by the song, despite, or perhaps because of, the happy rhythm that accompanied the sad tale and set it into sharp and painful relief. What manner of person would be able to sing of such difficulties with such a mixture of mockery and rue? Of humor and resolve? Who could contain such contradictions within himself without going mad?

"Well," I said. "Well, indeed." I cleared my throat.

Not long afterward, we said our good nights. I headed upstairs with the bottle and the glasses, set them in the kitchen, and tried to tease out some scenario by which this brilliant and unusual young man could be induced to stay. I would get a message to Rochester, and I would think of a few other options.

In bed I drifted off on a lake, asleep, and found myself in a forest of straw, with the sense that a fire was consuming some distant tract and I needed to make my way quickly. As I did so I was compelled to discard my effects, and I jettisoned a series of indistinct objects, which were then spirited away by unrecognizable creatures. Sometime in the night I was awakened from this dream, or vision, by a sound, a scraping sound of some sort, coming from outside the house. It seemed to persist, and I shook off the residue of sleep, put on my robe, and went downstairs to see the cause, taking a good oil lamp with me.

I stood under our *porte cochère*, padded about some, and could discover no cause. Likely some animal, I thought, rummaging for food. Raccoons and possums ruled the nighttime hours. Sometimes the mornings as well. Or perhaps it was one of my dream creatures come to life. As there seemed nothing discoverable I went back inside, paused to listen at the door to the basement, heard nothing there, and went back to bed.

The next morning's skies were the color of gypsum dust; snowflakes swept past the window as I took my breakfast and drank my coffee. Nicholas had brought the paper in, as usual, and I perused it until I heard, once again, the scraping noise that had awakened me in the night, along with some indistinct voices, I stood to investigate. Something—I cannot say quite what—impelled me to walk to our second pantry and open a door, behind which I kept two rifles and a pistol. I picked up one of the rifles and made sure it was loaded; then, satisfied, I went back to the side door and opened it onto the chill air.

Just down the driveway I saw a man I did not recognize and, past him a way farther down our drive toward the street, two useless characters whom I did recognize from the town.

"Who are you?" I said.

The one nearer me seemed to laugh slightly, and said, "Oh, hi. You're Mr. Seward?"

He was a singularly unattractive piece of work, with a turned eye and a greasy-looking hat and coat, and his manner of address could hardly have been more rude.

"I am Senator Seward," I said.

"Sure," he said. "Sorry to disturb you, Senator. We heard that somebody we're looking for is hiding in your house." He smiled after he said this, as if he had delivered some piece of witty news. "I'll bet you know who I'm talking about."

Addie would tell you that I do have a temper. It does not flare up often, but when it is aroused it is frightening even to myself. Insolence, injustice, disrespect, will summon it from its shallow slumber, and it came upon me then with a force that demanded all my willpower to control. My grip had tightened around the rifle barrel, which I held by my side. I consciously relaxed it as much as I could.

"You," I hollered to the two men who stood uneasily at the end of the drive, under the elms. "Collins and Shea. Get on your way. Now." Without any further word they walked off at a good pace. I turned my focus to the figure in front of me. "You are trespassing upon my property," I said.

"Well," he said, "I'm hired to find stolen goods, Senator. Those men are my deputies . . ."

"Deputies!" I said. "As well deputize horse manure. Leave my property now and do not come back."

The smile again. "Well, not so fast, there, Mr. Seward. The law says you have to help me, and anybody who doesn't can get . . ."

"I am a United States senator," I told him. "I *write* the law. And the law is not intended to give free rein to vigilantes. I'm telling you a final time that you are on my property, and if you remain here, or return, I promise you an unhappy ending." I leveled my rifle at him. "Get going."

Behind me I heard Ella call my name, asking if everything were all right. I told her to go back to the kitchen.

"You're not going to shoot me in the back, are you, Senator?" the figure said, with an ugly smile.

I was, I believe, angrier than I had ever been in my life. "Sir, I will shoot you in your head and claim self-defense if you are not gone by my count of ten."

With a couple of steps backward he started moving off, and then he turned and headed down the drive without a backward glance. I stood there and watched him until he walked out of our gate and headed to the left, toward town. When I was satisfied that he was gone, I walked back inside and sat at the table, leaned the rifle against a chair, and tried to steady myself. Nicholas appeared, and I told him I was all right, and to replace the rifle in its rack, which he did. When I had control of myself, I rang and requested more coffee.

I composed a note to the Friend who had conducted our guest, to apprise him of the development, and then it occurred to me to wonder whether William had heard these goings-on. I rose, walked to the basement door, and went down the stairs, calling William's name. I heard no answer.

He was not in the room. The bed had been made, and the banjar was gone, along with his few other effects.

"William," I called out, again.

On the table where our glasses had set the night before were the Dickens volumes I had lent him, and on top of them a small sheet of paper with some handwriting, which read:

> thank you, senator. I will be all rite, don't worry. Please say thank you to Missus Senator and to Fanny for me. I'll show her the trick next time I see you all.—Wm.

I sat down on the bed. I looked around our basement, which had given temporary shelter to many others, and would again. To live at the grace of others' goodwill. To live life without ever having a place of your own. To hide in basements. That the law should sanction the hunting of men! That any man dare call another property!

That evening we ate our dinner silently, as if in mourning. What was there to say? Fanny was, of course, heartbroken. After we had put her to bed, Addie and I sat up in the parlor, quietly. She was knitting, and I tried to read but had little success. In our warm parlor, by lamplight, I felt the cold outside. I feel it still, and I fear for my country.

ACKNOWLEDGMENTS

Thanks to my editor, and friend, Cal Morgan, his invaluable assistant, Laura Brown, and my brilliant and loyal agent Amy Williams. Thanks to the MacDowell Colony, where this book was begun, and Sheila Pleasants and the Virginia Center for the Creative Arts, where much of it was written. Thanks to Elvis Costello, Jeff Rosen, David Gates, and Ry Cooder for encouragement and friendship along the way, and to the banjo brain trust—Jim Bollman, Pete Ross, Cece Conway, Tony Thomas, Bob Smakula, Greg Adams, Kevin Enoch, Paul Brown, Bob Carlin, Tony Trischka, Bob Winans, Dom Flemons, Peter Szego, and Adam Hurt—for much insight and for favors large and small.

To the memory of Mike Seeger, and to Alexia Smith, who did me the honor of inviting me to choose a couple of Mike's instruments for my own, one of which was the banjo that started me thinking about the scenes, themes, and meanings that came together in this book.

To my mother, Lillian Piazza, who has always encouraged me with her spirit and love.

And, always, to Mary Howell, my much, much better half.

P.S.

Insights,
Interviews
& More . . .

About the author

About the book

Read on

Meet Tom Piazza

TOM PIAZZA is widely celebrated both as a novelist and as a writer on American music. His twelve books include the novels *A Free State* and *City of Refuge*, the post-Katrina manifesto *Why New Orleans Matters*, and the essay collection *Devil Sent the Rain: Music and Writing in Desperate America*. He was a principal writer for the innovative New Orleans–based HBO drama series *Treme*. His writing has appeared in *The New York Times*, *The Atlantic*, *Bookforum*, *The Oxford American*, and many other periodicals. He lives in New Orleans.

In both his fiction and his nonfiction, Piazza explores themes of cultural and personal identity, often using music as a prism through which to view American life. His 2015 novel *A Free State*, set in Virginia and Philadelphia just before the Civil War, explores the difficult, many-layered relationship between blackface minstrelsy and slavery, and the deep, painful, and still-contemporary riddles of race and society.

Piazza's 2008 novel *City of Refuge* follows the stories of two New Orleans families, one black and one white, during and after Hurricane Katrina; it was that year's One Book, One New Orleans selection, and it won the Willie Morris Award for Southern Fiction. His 2003 novel *My Cold War* won the Faulkner Society Award for the Novel, and his debut short-story collection *Blues and Trouble*, published in 1996, won the

James Michener Award. His book-length essay *Why New Orleans Matters*, published two and a half months after Hurricane Katrina in 2005, won the Louisiana Endowment for the Humanities' 2006 Humanities Book of the Year Award.

His writing on American music, including jazz, blues, country, and bluegrass, has been similarly recognized. He is a three-time winner of the ASCAP Deems Taylor Award for Music Writing (for his books *The Guide to Classic Recorded Jazz* and *Understanding Jazz*, and for his *Oxford American* column on Southern music), and in 2004 Piazza won a Grammy Award for his album notes to the five-CD set *Martin Scorsese Presents the Blues: A Musical Journey*. His music pieces have been widely anthologized, appearing in *Best Music Writing 2000*, *The Oxford American Book of Great Music Writing*, *Studio A: The Bob Dylan Reader*, and many other collections.

Piazza is a graduate of Williams College, and he holds an MFA in Fiction from the Iowa Writers' Workshop. In 2015 he received the Louisiana Writer Award from the Louisiana Center for the Book and the State Library of Louisiana, awarded annually to a writer "whose published body of work represents a distinguished and enduring contribution to the literary and intellectual heritage of Louisiana." ∾

That Was Now; This Is Then

Reproduced at the courtesy of the *Los Angeles Review of Books*, David Gates talks with Tom Piazza about *A Free State*.

Ever since I met Tom Piazza, some time in the early 2000s, we've been discovering random and not-so-random things we have in common: a tendency to overspend on Persian rugs, a fondness for the same books and music, an ability to quote verbatim speeches from *The Godfather* and imitate Yeats reading "The Lake Isle of Innisfree." We've drunk together, played country songs together—usually at the same time—we're both fiction writers (we've taught together), and we've both written extensively about music.

Tom's new novel, *A Free State*, involves the white leader of a blackface minstrel troupe in the 1850s and the genius black banjo player, an escaped slave, who joins the troupe in a double-switcheroo of racial impersonation. There's also a vicious and all-too-competent slave-catcher who's a hellhound on the banjo-player's trail, and a character about whom I'll say nothing, for fear of giving away a particularly bold novelistic move. No civilized person calls a book a "page-turner"—though e-book designers are surely working on eyeball-tracking technology that will render this horrible phrase a horrible reality—but *A Free State* certainly made *me* a page-turner—it didn't even allow me a coffee break. This short, tense novel distills Tom's perennial concerns—race and justice, music and creativity—and I wanted to talk with him about it.

—David Gates

DAVID GATES: Back when *A Free State* was just getting under way, you told me how you came up with the idea, and how you got your editor interested in the project. I'd never heard such a story, and I think everyone out there would like to hear it too.

TOM PIAZZA: A few years ago I started playing clawhammer banjo—another thing you and I have in common. I started reading about the history of the banjo, and you can't do that for long before it leads you right into both the history of slavery in the United States and the incredible phenomenon of blackface minstrelsy in the early and mid-nineteenth century. At the same moment that the national debate about slavery was coming to a boil, you also had this national sensation—white men smearing burnt cork on their faces and playing banjo and fiddle and tambourine and bones, singing and playing songs meant to be taken as "authentic Negro" performance. It was the rock and roll of pre–Civil War America.

Somewhere in the reading I ran across one of the countless advertisements that slave "owners" would place, offering rewards for their escaped slaves. These ads always included detailed physical descriptions—identifying marks, clothing, height, characteristics of their speech, all that. But this ad I saw also described the runaway as being "very proficient on the banjar [banjo] and likely to have one with him." And I thought, what a tragic situation—this man had the talent to be recognized as a musician, as well as the spirit and resourcefulness to get free, and suddenly the music he loves, the thing that is his source of self-definition, not to mention a source of earnings, is now a giant target on his back. His greatest strength is his greatest vulnerability.

That image and that situation stuck with me, and I thought ▶

5

That Was Now; This Is Then *(continued)*

I might have to do something with it some day. But I had just spent three years writing for HBO's *Treme*, and working on material for a completely different novel, and that image of the escapee and the price of his freedom just went underground in my mind, waiting.

Late that year I showed my editor some of the material for the other novel I'd been working on, and he wasn't wild about it. It just wasn't to his taste. So I talked to my agent, who said, "Well, do you have anything else?" I told her that I did have a germinal idea, but, it was really nothing, I said, just an image. She pressed me to tell her about it, and I started talking about the escaped slave, and within about fifteen minutes the entire book was there, in principle and in outline. It had been taking shape without my realizing it.

GATES: Obviously this minstrel music was never recorded, but I found myself wondering what it must have sounded like. Do you have any guesses? Might it have resembled the recordings we've got of black fiddle-banjo music from the first half of the twentieth century—ensembles like the Sid Hemphill band, recorded by Alan Lomax, which, as I recall, has a drum in addition to fiddle, banjo, and guitar? Or, since these *were* white people playing the music, maybe it was more like white fiddle-banjo music—the sort of thing Tommy Jarrell and Fred Cockerham played? Or, since these were more or less *urban* white musicians, and obviously from an earlier time, might it have sounded less raw? What might these white minstrels have heard, and how would they have adapted it to the ears and sensibilities of their audiences, as well as to their own?

PIAZZA: Well, as you imply, it's impossible to know exactly. The closest we can get to hearing what those early minstrel ensembles might have sounded like is a recording by a professor named Robert Winans. He assembled a classic minstrel line, with the banjo, fiddle, tambourine, and bones, figured out an appropriate repertoire, and made the disc *The Early Minstrel Show*. Some of the lyrics are extremely offensive, but you can't look at minstrelsy without being honest about the brutal racism involved.

More recently, a banjo player named Tim Twiss made it his business to record every tune in the main banjo instruction books printed in the 1850s and 1860s—just solo banjo music in the so-called "stroke" style used by the minstrel players, which was the precursor to clawhammer style. He put it all on a flash drive and calls it "Early Banjo Complete." I think it gives the best answer to your question, which is that the early style was apparently a hash of different styles. Some of the tunes sound like a kind of proto-ragtime, syncopated and, to my ears, clearly African-American-derived. Other tracks are really Irish fiddle tunes transcribed for banjo—jigs and reels. Most of them show the influence of both streams. From the beginning, American music depended on that tension between African-derived elements and European-derived elements.

GATES: Whatever it sounded like, obviously white performers, like your narrator, as well as white audiences found energy, joy, release—call it what you will—in this music. Their caricatured impersonations of shiftless, chicken-stealing, (etc., etc.) blacks reek of contempt to us, yet there also seems to be a strong element of wish-fulfilling fantasy—as if the performers wanted to be (I'll use a deliberately paradoxical word) as "free" as those blacks whom they were imagining as tricksters rather than sufferers. This sort of fantasy, of course, didn't die out with minstrelsy. I'm thinking of Norman Mailer's essay "The White Negro" and of Lou Reed's offensively ironic/ironically offensive song "I Wanna Be Black." And of 80 kajillion other examples. Your novel takes place during what seems to be an important moment in the evolution of this central weirdness in American ideation. Could you talk some about that moment— what had come before, what was to come later, and what it might have been like living in it?

PIAZZA: *A Free State* is my best imagining of what it might have been like "living in it" at that time. But, you know, we are still living in it. I don't think of this as a historical novel. That bizarre transaction you talk about in the question is still with us, right? You hear a white college kid calling his pal "homey," ▶

or a soccer mom call her husband "dawg"—where's the difference?

The novel is about freedom and what people imagine it to be, what they are willing to pay for it, and how they like what they have after they get it. It's never what you think it's going to be— just like fame, or turning twenty-one. Enslaved Africans did, in fact, find all kinds of ways of claiming freedom for themselves even within that monstrous system, and music is one of the most recognizable. "Free" white people, listening to that musical expression, often recognized it as a particular form of freedom (as you point out) and, I would think, experienced some degree of envy, along with whatever else they were experiencing. But the freedom in that musical expression was often mistaken for simple happiness. Such happiness is never simple, but there were, and are, strong psychological reasons in a lot of white minds for wanting it to be. It absolves those minds of guilt, for one thing. So does the relentless, viciously cynical depiction that we have today of black people as thugs and gangstas. You know: "Either they don't mind their enslavement, or they are such brutes that they deserve it."

GATES: Right, right—"The past isn't even past," as Uncle Willie Faulkner said. On the other hand, you could argue that almost any novel is an historical novel—your own *City of Refuge* imagines a moment in history, no matter how small the gap in time between Hurricane Katrina and your writing the book. Or would you argue that *no* novel is an historical novel? How would you define that genre? Who practices it? Hilary Mantel? Gore Vidal? Mailer, in something like *Ancient Evenings*? Is it just a dismissive term? Dickens's *A Tale of Two Cities* and *Barnaby Rudge* are set in the eighteenth century—historical novels or not? How about *Great Expectations*, which seems to be set decades before Dickens wrote it? Is that disqualified as an historical novel simply because it doesn't deal with large public events, like the French Revolution or the Gordon riots? Are there novels you had somewhere in the back of your mind as you wrote *A Free State*? Not necessarily as templates or inspirations— nothing that direct or explicit—but just novels that might have

been kicking around that made you think maybe you weren't so crazy, and that this really was a novel and not some delusional project? I ask because I'm prone to such doubts when I'm writing and because I find it difficult to compare *A Free State* to anything else I've read.

PIAZZA: I think a historical novel is one in which the history itself is the point. Readers are supposedly invited, or guided, through a window into a distant, or not-so-distant, time, where they meet famous people and take a little vacation from present reality. Or if there are no famous people, at least they get to be in a clearly branded Somewhere Else for the duration of the book; in that way it is distancing and comforting. The material is behind glass, no matter how well imagined. It's a form of tourism. And it's comforting to the extent that you know it's over. You know— "Wow—I just spent three days at the court of Marie Antoinette. What a bunch of knuckleheads!" Or "I just spent the most marvelous four hundred pages with Theodore Roosevelt!"

There's history, and then there's the past. History is, by definition, over with; it's a construct, but the conceit is that the author is trying to give his or her best shot at telling you how it was. That's the payoff. But Faulkner is right—the past, by contrast, lives with us and disturbs us still because it is full of unfinished business. You know Thomas Mann's short story "Disorder and Early Sorrow"? The main character is a history professor trying to keep his family's life together during that post–World War I time when Germany's economy had completely fallen apart and all the social models were breaking down. And in the middle of that, "history" is this comforting refuge for the professor. One of the all-time great stories. You could do a great classroom sequence reading that back-to-back with *The Sound and the Fury*.

Joan Didion has always set her fiction against some urgent sociopolitical context, but I wouldn't call her novels "historical." You could take a book like Robert Stone's *Dog Soldiers*, which is ostensibly about the Vietnam War, but it disturbs you because it is showing these perennial dark strains in the human spirit. I wouldn't call it a historical novel. I wouldn't call *A Farewell to* ▶

Arms a historical novel; the fighting comes to the foreground, recedes, comes forward, recedes . . . It's about the nature of experience, not about the specifics of a given war. In a funny way I think a book like *Ragtime*, for all its modernist and post-modernist tropes, is more of a historical novel than either of those. You don't want history to sit on the character elements so heavily that they get smothered.

But anyway, I don't think *A Free State* is a historical novel. I see no distance between the dynamics of what goes on in my book and the dynamics of contemporary life. That being said, I did a lot of reading on certain topics—slavery and slave-hunters, blackface minstrelsy, nineteenth-century Philadelphia—because I wanted to be faithful to the factual aspects of the place and moment I chose; I didn't want to skew reality by mixing up what was possible and what was not possible at that time. Everything in *A Free State* is possible. But to me that's not the payoff; it's just, like, the table ante. In a historical novel it's the payoff.

GATES: I think what you're saying is that the term "historical novel" is, or has become, code for pop junk. But of course I can think of any number of works, set in the historical past and with famous historical figures, which are legitimately disturbing, full of unfinished business, and which deal with recognizable human beings—Shakespeare's history plays? I suspect you simply don't want your book to be easily categorized and dismissed, and I don't blame you. I guess for me it comes down to the question of whether or not a book is any good.

A Free State is largely written in a nineteenth-century voice, but—unlike the conventional "historical novel"—it's not an imitation of nineteenth-century fiction. On the other hand, it doesn't seem especially radical (by twentieth-century modernist standards) in its shifts of narrative viewpoint and technique—until we get near the end, where you make a headsnapping move, which we probably ought not to discuss in detail for fear of spoiling it for those who haven't yet read the book. That move gave me a twofold jolt. On a purely technical level, it put me on notice that this really *was* a fully contemporary novel, which sought to subvert my generic expectations. And that subversion seemed to have thematic implications—this is material that allows no comfortable resting place. The very last sentence—again, I'm being deliberately evasive—seems to catapult the reader into the present, and (God help us) even into the future. It's a last line, and it resonates as a last line should, but it's perhaps the opposite of an ending.

Is this what you wanted to happen to the reader? Is this what happened to you as you were writing it?

PIAZZA: "No resting place" is correct, and I guess I see that, ultimately, as the price of freedom. The material shouldn't allow a comfortable resting place, because that is the thematic and technical understructure of the book. Freedom—whether it involves shifting identity, geographical mobility, creative activity—entails constant escape from the given. I think that's one of the reasons we both find Bob Dylan's career so vitalizing; he constantly slips the yoke of the given and of people's expectations. You pay a price, though.

But I'm still thinking about what you said about historical novels. To the extent that they are "legitimately disturbing" and "full of unfinished business," I would resist calling them "historical" novels. They are imagined works, and as soon as a given character is really imagined so that he or she becomes a living, complex organism on the page, that character is a fictional creation, no longer a historical figure. And to the extent that you are trying to serve the historical model, present the supposed historical model rather than transforming the model into something of your own, the work will be weak as fiction. This is how I see it, anyway.

You bring up Shakespeare's "historical" plays . . . I wouldn't call them "histories," no matter what Shakespeare or anybody else calls them. Not the great ones, anyway. Because the point is not really to serve a literal history or bring you face to face with some putatively real historical figure. Nobody reads or watches *King Lear* to find out about the historical model for that character of King Lear. And the proof that these are not historical plays, in the sense that I was discussing "historical novels," is that the best have been so perennially adaptable into so many contexts other that the supposed historical one. You know—*King Lear* as a ▶

newspaper tycoon, or whatever. As we all know, they are constantly being recast in different historical periods and cultural contexts. If they were really about the history they'd never be recast in that way.

GATES: You tricky bastard, bringing up *King Lear*—whom I'd call a semi-legendary figure. Let's see you wriggle out of a discussion of the two parts of *Henry IV* and *Henry V* without reference to history. And I mean capital-H History. Seems to me the other Uncle Willie had historical-political stuff on his mind, in addition to the "Godfather"-like father-son story, and all the other "timeless" personal/human/whatever goings-on. I don't mean to get you into a ring with Mr. Tolstoy (or Mr. Shakespeare), but can't a sufficiently big novel take on both? Or would you rather talk about *The Godfather* and its obvious source in *Henry IV*? I'm making you an offer you can't refuse. I do grant your point about the many decontextualized versions of Shakespeare, which I imagine (based on nothing but my own wishes) he would have liked.

PIAZZA: So now you have "slander'd me with bastardy." (*King John*, Act 1; scene 1). Okay, look, to paraphrase Desdemona, "Oh Lord, please don't let me be misunderstood." Obviously, I'm not saying that bringing in historical figures or recognizable events tied to a given time makes a novel cheesy, or that fictional narrative should float free of historical context. How could I possibly say that, given the setting and action of *A Free State*, not to mention *City of Refuge* and *My Cold War*? But that's different from what I'm talking about. I say that if a novel—or a film or a play; or a painting, for that matter—is serious, the interesting dimension doesn't lie in delivering some faithful account of the factual historical record, or the character of Eleanor Roosevelt, or Stonewall Jackson. Or Henry V or Julius Caesar. Anyone who goes to see *Julius Caesar* to learn history is . . . misinformed. Obviously, Shakespeare makes use—*his* use—of events and characters, and he alters them as he wishes. You can't learn the history of the Spanish Civil War by looking at *Guernica*, although the painting is obviously tied to that bombing, and you don't need to know about the events that inspired the painting to feel its impact. Tolstoy, since you bring him up, might be as close as you could get to somebody who really did both, but you don't read *War and Peace* because you want to learn about the Franco-Russian conflict, although you will certainly learn about those events from reading it. You read it because you dig Tolstoy's vision of events and characters. Same with Dickens, sir. The measure of good novels' success is not how close they bring us to some imagined golden mean of historical faithfulness. I can't imagine that you'd disagree. But I think that is what so-called "historical novels" look to deliver. You know—*Creek of Blood! A Novel of Antietam*, or *Panzer! A Novel of 1943*. Or *Dead Queens Don't Wear Plaid—A Novel of Mary, Queen of Scots*.

The imagination has to get free of whatever limits it in the writing, including preconceptions about historical figures' personality or motives. Just as Henry, in *A Free State*, has to get free of all these external definitions, whether they're applied to him by slave "owners," or abolitionists, or audiences. . . .

GATES: Okay, agreed. I've only been goading you to see if you'd make the distinctions you're making. As I might have known you would. I don't really have a dog in this fight, since I'd never read—much less write—something like *Creek of Blood*. Though I wish I'd thought up the title.

I trust it's not giving too much away to say that much of the tension in the novel comes from the pursuit of a runaway slave by a brutal, dogged, and apparently all-too-competent slave-catcher. I worried throughout about what was going to happen—by the way, I consider getting the reader worried a positive accomplishment—and I wondered if you knew all along how it would come out. If you didn't, at what point *did* you know? (Or "decide," if that's how you experience the working-out of a story.) If you did know all along, or from early on, how did you keep yourself interested enough in the uncertainty to make it convincing?

PIAZZA: I did not know all along what would happen, and I can't recall exactly when I did know. Pretty close to when it happened. ▸

That Was Now; This Is Then *(continued)*

But even when you know in principle, you still may not know the exact way it will play out. As you say, you have to keep yourself interested. In my view, events have to come out of the characters; the characters can't be forced to conform to an advance template of events. And everyone, or almost everyone, in the book has such mixed motives; things are always kind of up in the air until they happen. So you just have to listen carefully every step of the way to hear what's really going on, as opposed to what you think should go on. Just like life, right?

GATES: About what I suspected—it certainly felt discovered rather than contrived, like Flannery O'Connor's surprise at the Bible salesman's stealing Hulga's artificial leg as she was writing "Good Country People." (Should I have said "Spoiler alert"?) Though I guess I'm susceptible to having my chain jerked by a cleverly contrived contrivance. I'll ask a similar question about the one horrifically brutal scene in the novel—I'm sure you know the one I'm talking about. Did this just happen as you were writing the scene? Seems to me this moment resonates in the book well after it's happened—I never quite got over it—which I assume is what you wanted. Yet as I recall, you hit such a note only once. In a novel set in the days of slavery, though not principally set on a plantation, how much brutality is enough, too much, not enough?

PIAZZA: It depends on what you're trying to achieve, I guess. That brutal scene you mention followed from the character of Tull, the slave hunter, as I understood him, and what I knew of the times and circumstances. . . . Once it happens, you know what Tull is capable of, and that's really all you need. I think there's a natural tendency to overdo it when you're trying to render something as hideous as the enslavement of human beings. It's never enough, because the pain and injustice are bottomless. If you try to compete with the reality by piling on more and more incident and detail, horror upon horror, you'll end up diminishing the picture rather than strengthening it. Better to underplay and let the reader fill in some blanks. Part of the real horror of that time and that system was how *normal* that stuff came to feel to the perpetrators of the crime, on the surface at least. They considered themselves respectable gentry, men of business, an aristocracy. Tull doesn't do his work out of hatred for the enslaved people. I think he dislikes the slave-owning class more than he dislikes the slaves themselves. But he considers himself a professional. What he can't stand is any form of resistance or implied disrespect, or what he would interpret as disrespect. A little switch can get thrown and he is capable of anything. But he thinks of himself as completely reasonable, and in fact better than everybody around him, when it comes right down to it. He's a real psychopath.

GATES: Hmm. A professional who can't stand resistance or disrespect? A little switch gets thrown and he's capable of anything? I've been following the news out of Ferguson, Charleston, and wherever else. Shall I say the obvious?

PIAZZA: Well, I think you just did. As I said, I don't think of this as a historical novel. And it's worth remembering that Tull and his kind were operating technically within the law as it stood at the time. Most of the world-class thugs of the past and present have used the cover of law, whether secular or religious, to claim sanction for what they do. But this is a novel, not a political tract. Finally, it comes down to individuals and what they make of their circumstances, for good or for ill. Usually, since these are human beings, for both. ⌒

Books of Further Interest

The following are some books that will be worthwhile to anyone who finds the situations, themes, and contexts of *A Free State* interesting.

BLACKFACE MINSTRELSY AND EARLY AFRICAN-AMERICAN MUSIC

BLACKING UP: THE MINSTREL SHOW IN NINETEENTH-CENTURY AMERICA
by Robert Toll
....

Pioneering overview of the blackface minstrel phenomenon. The place to start for the basic history of minstrelsy.

LOVE AND THEFT: BLACKFACE MINSTRELSY AND THE AMERICAN WORKING CLASS
by Eric Lott
....

Powerfully argued and well-researched book on the social, economic, race, and class issues surrounding, and woven into, blackface minstrelsy and its audience's responses to it. Stimulating, essential reading.

DEMONS OF DISORDER: EARLY BLACKFACE MINSTRELS AND THEIR WORLD
by Dale Cockrell
....

Worthwhile, somewhat scattershot examination not just of blackface but other forms of ritual masking in nineteenth-century popular culture. Less intellectually rigorous than Eric Lott's *Love and Theft*, but worth reading.

SINFUL TUNES AND SPIRITUALS: BLACK FOLK MUSIC TO THE CIVIL WAR
by Dena J. Epstein

There is no way to have a full understanding of African-American musical traditions and their influence without reading this book. From the earliest reports of African music in the Americas pre-1800, through the specifics of the slaves' musical instruments, through black secular and religious music of all types, this book is a triumph and a classic.

THE BANJO ITSELF

AMERICA'S INSTRUMENT: THE BANJO IN THE 19TH CENTURY
by Philip F. Gura and James F. Bollman

Lavishly illustrated history following the banjo from its earliest, simplest forms through its rise as a central instrument in American popular music. The book also provides a fascinating angle from which to view the development of American means of manufacturing from individual craftsmen, through workshops, to factories and mass production. Thoroughly enjoyable and very useful.

BANJO: AN ILLUSTRATED HISTORY
by Bob Carlin

If you have room for only one banjo book on your shelf, this should be it. Beautifully illustrated, intelligently organized, and very readable, this coffee-table prize traces the instrument's ▶

history from its earliest incarnations up through today, viewing it through the lenses of technology, music, popular culture, prominent performers, and even collectors, always with an emphasis on the banjo's beauty and expressive possibilities. Essential.

THE BANJO: AMERICA'S AFRICAN INSTRUMENT
by Laurent Dubois

Fascinating and authoritative history of the banjo going back to its roots in Africa and its dissemination through the Americas, by a serious scholar.

THE BIRTH OF THE BANJO: JOEL WALKER SWEENEY AND EARLY MINSTRELSY
by Bob Carlin

Part biography of the pioneer blackface banjo performer, part meticulously researched window into the earliest days of minstrelsy, this excellent short book is readable and historically reliable. Author Bob Carlin is himself one of the preeminent contemporary banjo performers.

STRATEGIES AND TACTICS OF ESCAPE

UNDERGROUND RAILROAD: AUTHENTIC NARRATIVES AND FIRST-HAND ACCOUNTS
by William Still

William Still was an African-American businessman in Philadelphia and the key figure in that city's very active Underground Railroad network. When escaped slaves would arrive at his office, a principal stop on the way to Canada and freedom, Still would interview them about their lives and their escape. The narratives he collected may be seen as the first American oral histories, and they are an astonishing human testament. Absolutely essential reading.

THE GREAT ESCAPES: FOUR SLAVE NARRATIVES
INTRODUCTION AND NOTES
by Daphne A. Brooks

As the subtitle indicates, this book collects four narratives, written by former slaves about their early lives and how they escaped. Invaluable for a sense of the lives led by enslaved Africans in America, told from the inside, as well as a stunning look at the daring and ingenuity employed in their escapes. Includes not one but two narratives by Henry "Box" Brown, who had himself shipped from Newport News, Virginia, to William Still's Pennsylvania office in a wooden crate.

RUNAWAY SLAVES: REBELS ON THE PLANTATION
by John Hope Franklin and Loren Schweninger

Invaluable and definitive work examining every aspect of life for runaways and those charged with bringing them back. Very readable, full of fascinating detail and anecdote, simultaneously heartbreaking and inspiring.

BOOKS BY TOM PIAZZA

DEVIL SENT THE RAIN
Music and Writing in Desperate America

Available in Paperback and Ebook

"Filled with energy and tender, insightful words
for the brilliant and irascible.... He identifies the
unlikely, precious connections between recent events,
art, letters, and music." —Elvis Costello

CITY OF REFUGE
A Novel

Available in Paperback and Ebook

"A classic . . . a book timeless in its ability
to go right to the heart of certain values
that have filled the lives of individuals
throughout our history." —*Denver Post*

WHY NEW ORLEANS MATTERS

Available in Paperback and Ebook

**Contains new material to commemorate the
ten year anniversary of Hurricane Katrina**

"Explains far better than I ever could why people
love New Orleans and why all of us should care
about its salvation."
—*Newsweek*

MY COLD WAR
A Novel

Available in Paperback

"There's a painful, penetrating authenticity . . .
Reveals the depth of [Piazza's] perceptiveness
and talent." —*New York Times Book Review*